Stonefish

Stonefish

Keri Hulme

First published in 2004 by Huia Publishers,
39 Pipitea Street, PO Box 17-335,
Wellington, Aotearoa New Zealand.
www.huia.co.nz

ISBN 1-869690-88-5

National Library of New Zealand Cataloguing-in-Publication Data
Hulme, Keri.
Stonefish / Keri Hulme.
ISBN 1-869691-06-7 (hbk.) — 1-869690-88-5 (pbk.)
I. Title.
NZ823.2—dc 22

Cover photograph by Justin Spiers

Mō taku hākui, mō Mary A. Miller, me te whānau katoa,
me Te Naybore – even after a quarter century! – Judith Maloney

Remembering the Dead

William G. R. Miller
Raymond D. Miller
David M. Miller

Alan Jolis
Robin Morrison
William P.C.J. Minehan
Irihapeti M. Ramsden

Contents

'I have a stone that once swam
ancient seas' – it lies
big eyed, gills agasp
thin as varnish on the shale
only lacquer left from life.

I am a fish
familiar of these seas
of deadly air and
I know the knife of age and
I know stone –

On this finger another ancient swimmer
flash flicker flares greenlightningblue:
you smile at my rocks
but I murmur opals; you
say ancestors and I breathe,
Bones –

Floating Words

THINKING BACK
(I am balanced on the end bollard, the slip-rope in my hand) there were omens all along.

For example, quite early on, before anything began to move, a kingfisher perched on the powerlines, a sprat in its bill. Kingfishers quite often perch on powerlines, but this one stayed there all day. The sprat kept twitching – at least, every time I looked out and saw the kingfisher still there, the sprat would spasm again. All of us who were here, then, noticed the bird and the fish, and we all commented on it, but none of us wondered about it in depth. None of us saw the kingfisher fly away, either. Presumably the sprat was eventually swallowed.

THERE WAS ALSO the last time I picked mushrooms.

It had been drizzling for days. Normally the mid-year is rain-time, two or three inches a day, a night, but the weather turned lazy. Endless days masked in misty feeble drizzle. So I had put off going out for mushrooms, and put off and put off until one day my hunger for them overcame my sense. Our mushroom fields are – were – different. It's Agaricales here, bitorquis and subperonatus mainly, but occasionally a broad fat arvensis, eagerly sought for because of its rich taste. They grow along the airstrip, half a mile of sheep-shorn grass, and throughout the picnic areas. Even then, the sea edging in from the south had whittled the picnic areas away, and the remaining knobs of sheep dung on the strip had a sad grey patina to them. The sheep themselves had been trucked away, weeks before.

I amble along the strip, seemingly aimlessly. When I first went gathering, I would mistake driftwood and pallid stones and old gnawed bits of sheepbone for mushrooms, because I made the mistake of *looking* for them. That was years ago; now I have my eye in. Now I wander, humming quietly. There is a rusty brown cap, barely thumbnail-sized; there is a handwide parasol; here is a clutch of beauties, their tops pale as eggs. I have nearly a bag full when I stop midway down the strip.

There is a thick white mist, north, and I can no longer see Abut Head. The mail-blimp said it has retreated, two mile or more she said. The Tasman runs fierce and wild just over a new stonebank; it has come in another chain since I was here last.

I sigh: Change, change, change. Where is solidity? Where is the rock?

Turning south again to finish gathering from the strip, my eye is caught by something odd-looking, wrong, out-of-place. A burst of colour by a clump of toetoe. It looks, upon examination, like a bolete – well, it has that family's spongy tissue under the cap – but it is coloured like no bolete I have ever heard of. There is a repulsive fungus from Haast called *Tylopilus formosus*, which is brown-black on top, and a horrid livid pink undercap; there is a variety of *Hygrophorus* named 'multicolour' which is red and green and sulphur yellow *outside*, and turquoise blue *inside*. This thing looks like a mismatch between them. Greeny black on top, and blue underneath, and red and yellow in alternate bands up the length of the stalk.

No way am I going to eat it, but I want to know more about it, so I disengage it from the sand with care, and weave a swift rough kete from toetoe leaves to bear it home. And bear it home on bleeding fingers I do: not for nothing is toetoe known as cutty-grass.

In the misty distance is a shy retreating figure, a grey shadow in the drizzle. Though there are so few of us left, it makes no move towards me. That is understandable. Mushroom-pickers are solitary creatures, and don't like other mushroom-pickers too close.

I REMEMBER THAT the mushroom caps were slightly slimy from the continuous drizzle, and that there was more sand than usual in the gills. Cooking them: half a cup of extra virgin olive oil, salt, two crushed cloves of garlic, and a lot of shredded parsley (my herbs transferred surprisingly well to buckets and terracotta pots upstairs) … add the mushrooms, and let all stew. A relishsome mix, that would be perfect with bacon chunks.

There hasn't been bacon available – or any meat – for months.

THERE WERE NO abnormal dreams that I recall. Flood dreams, yes: but everybody had those, conjured by the news reports (while transmission lasted).

I feel there should have been intimations of what was going on, shadows and forebodings. To the contrary: my dreams were peaceful and curiously green/rustic/waterless.

THEN THERE WAS the visitor.

Now, she was a sign of the times to come if ever there was one.

It was quite early on, after the water began rising, before the bubble cities came. I'd been writing hard, because the mail-blimp system was well-established and dependable. I never did find out who started it, how credit was established, but it worked:

'I need

- flour (stone-ground, organically-grown, from Kaikoura)
- cheese (Hipi-mā, please)
- oil (olive, and avocado)
- shoyu
- cider vinegar (Healtheries) and
- dried apricots (any left from Roxburgh?)

Herewith chapter 23.'

And the mail-blimp received note and chapter, and handed over last week's order (Motueka tobacco, and NiuGinea blue-mountain beans, and a crate of Havill's Mazer Mead). The more detailed the order, the better your chances of getting anything. For some reason, never divulged, you would only receive processed food or drink. No fresh fruit or vegetables: no meat (not even salami). And if no writing accompanied the order, all that came back was a small recycled-cardboard box, with an exclamation mark made of pāua-shell inside. Someone out there had a sense of humour. I only tried to gain credit without payment of words, once …

Anyway, I had been writing hard, all that day, most of the evening. After twenty hours at it, I was as March roes on a flounder, blackened, emptied, sour. In a mood only for a bottle of mead, and then to bed and oblivion. I'd finished 47, and got this far on the opening of the tangihanga chapter (not the end one, as you might think, but the beginning of the second section):

> The coffin was really starting to brew.
>
> The strong midday sun, of course, and the fact that they hadn't found him before the river had kept him for a week: the morgue people had done their best but it clearly wasn't enough to offset the work of the eels and the water, and it wasn't going to be sufficient to keep him together for the whole three days.

Good enough for starters, I thought, and then there's a knock on the door.

– Who is it?

Silence.

– Who *is* it?

More silence. Then the knock, tat-tat-tat BAM, three times the knuckles and once the open hand, *my* knock damn it (my pulse quickening), redoubled in force.

Piss on you too, I think, but it is the fag-end of a hard day, and it would be nicer to share a bottle of mead with a guest, than drink it in moody solitude.

I check that the cutdown .410 is there, ready on the back of the door (it is) and the waddy is waiting to one side (it is), and then I slide the dead-bolt.

She says, in a voice full of disappointment,

– You're fatter than I thought you'd be.

I stand there, gawping.

– Bit of a sag-belly too eh?

and pushes past, headed straight for my grog cabinet.

Her hand brings out the bottle of Lagavulin without hesitation, although it is cunningly hidden by a row of other, lesser, single malts, and she knows exactly where I keep my scotch glasses, in a cupboard in the desk. She even picks out my favourite one before sprawling down on the best chair.

– You still got your fridge in the garage? Get us a bottle of milk eh?

– Rup bup bup …

Well, even I'd ignore that sort of noise.

She's started singing,

O yeah so I bear
the stigmata
of the hard drinker
a doer a goer
a wine-cup thinker – still
will you barter
your dreams for
mine?

O I know that song, 'Wine-song #33', early one of a long-running unpublished series …

– Milk eh?

There is a subtle menacing emphasis on that last 'eh?' It is exactly the subtle menacing emphasis I use myself when some younger member of the family group has grown tiresomely obtuse. It warns, You don't oblige/get your act together *immediately*, someone round here is going to regret what happens next.

I'd just love to see you try, woman! I outweigh you by, o I'd say a stone and a half … but your hands have that tough corded look mine lost years ago. And you look meaner, as well as leaner. So we won't try fisticuffs. Yet.

She's smiling a mean lean smile.

I go out and get the milk (which comes in plastic sachets, these days. Interesting, I suddenly think, remembering 'still got your fridge in the garage?' Even in this dazed state that is sufficient to suggest time lags.) I grab my last bottle of Lindauer's finest. Ultra Brut Cuvee Sans Dosage. That's about as mean, and lean, a champagne as you'll get, anywhere.

I can already see, despite disbelief – it's like reality has sneezed, and split – it is going to be one of those occasions where sober straight forward action will get me nowhere.

The winter moon that night was very pale.

'A pale moon doth rain.'

A LONG TIME AGO, when I first started coining whakataukī-waina, aphorisms that could be, or become, proverbial sayings, I had as my initial effort:

'When you are drowning, the depth of the water is of last concern.'

The essential requirement of a whakataukī-waina is that it seems to make sense – it *does* make sense, a kind of sense, but that sense is edgy and changeable, and if you think too much about it, you step into mental quicksand, skiddy and sinking all at once. That's why they're *wine* proverbs, not too much use or good anywhen else.

Auē! Whakataukī-waina; my family group; the last bottle of Lindauer, and the comparatively easy task of dealing with an imaginary clone of myself turned real. It all seems so remote and innocent these days …

THEN, OF COURSE, I thought the world had gone mad.

There I was, drowning in unreality, and the depth of the wine the last concern.

Half a bottle gone, half a bottle to go. There she sits, sipping whisky curds, feet propped up on a stool, sharkskin boots too close to my thigh. She wears her hair plaited in a short thick club covering the back of her neck. She has seven silver rings on her fingers, and her shirt is earth-red. The kilt is new, hand-woven hodden, with no elaborate pleats, a simple drape and fold secured by a thin black belt. The kilt is different: I hadn't ever visualised the kilt.

– You're staying long? My query sounds desperate. I am desperate.

She smiles evilly, and adds more whisky to the clabber.

– What brought you here? I mean, from – there? and she just flicks out her ball lightning, the personal charge every woman in that fantasy of mine carried, flicks out a tiny part of her lightning at a passing mosquito and zapples it dead.

IT COULD HAVE BEEN disastrous: it could have been my end. After I'd got rid of Kei-Tu, I became very leery about who I fantasised: it was one thing putting people down on paper, quite another to have them lying, vomit-covered and comatose drunk on the floor (a whole bottle of Lagavulin, even when ruined by two litres of milk, does that to the most hardened drinker). I remembered that shadowy person I had seen while mushroom-picking: about my height, about my size. The skittery way it moved. Could it have been the Weever, with her monochromatic tattoos and blank assassin's eyes? I shuddered. I had invented too many characters I wouldn't want to meet. When I wrote my chapters now, to earn the daily bread (polenta/straw mushrooms/lentils), I avoided detail, intensity, realism … it didn't seem to matter to whoever – or whatever – read them at the other end.

IT WAS ABOUT THIS TIME that my neighbour Lux Malone broke down her top-storey and turned it into a giant square raft, like a cattle ferry. She built a small A-frame house upon it, and left the rest of the raft to the oyster spat she imported. The oysters grew, and spawned, and grew. She poles her oyster farm from the remaining houses, to the fortified village that juts over the swamp bay, to that eerie half-submerged colony of dirt-coloured domes which appeared overnight where the wharf-shed used to be, and trades oysters for what we have to offer.

She says, only a wet-suited arm ever comes out of the dome-colony hatch. She says, they produce interesting syrups. She says, all the men have now shifted into the fortified village, and have started a long-house culture there. Even Bond. She scowls.

Bond had been her mate.

I say quickly,

– Have you noticed other changes?

She scratches her thigh thoughtfully. She is leaning on the long mānuka pole she uses to shift around her oyster farm.

– I heard they are catching blue-eyed kōura up the hill.

– Do they do anything? The kōura I mean? Smarter, or more dangerous?

– Nah, sweeter …

Her tribe of gathered-in children skitter around the oyster farm in pirogues as sharp and swift as flick-knives. Their voices are sweet and high, but their words are unintelligible. I swap her a bunch of dried thyme and a small bottle of ngaio oil for keeping the sandflies at bay, and get a sack of oysters.

– See you, Lux …

– Yeah, see you –

But we probably won't. Our worlds are drifting further apart.

THE TIDE HAS reached my front fence, and the porch is dancing with a thousand whirling leaves from the dying peppermint gum. Ah wind, blow the mists away …

I continue creosoting the bottom storey. I have put on four coats already, and the fumes make for heady working, but more is needed. Creosote is going to be the only thing that will keep the lower portion of the house from rotting as the water rises. I have shifted all the books upstairs – the rooms there stand twelve feet above what used to be the ground. I have made a sign, FREE LIBRARY, and left the seaward door unlocked.

I've also left all the gear I won't be taking out on a raft by the gate. As I wade out with another armload (two Rust pots, an early Colin McCahon, and four spare duvets), I see that the pile is diminishing. Someone takes it away, the men from the fortified village, maybe the arms from the domes. Perhaps it is just the tide.

The barge is nearly ready: I've used the boards from the erstwhile high fence round my house (I turn the fenceposts into bollards). They are treated kahikatea, long-lasting in water and easy to work. It's a large barge, thirty-six feet long and twenty feet wide. Working slowly, steadily, I transfer my main living room onto it. I become experienced with pulleys and levers, and don't have much trouble, even with the York Seal range. Indeed, the only trouble I've had shifting things has been with the lemon bush and the Cox's Orange apple tree: they sulked when first wrenched, and stubbornly refuse to flourish now, despite being in great wicker baskets with rich soil and room for their roots to spread. Never mind:

they'll get used to the fact that nothing is static, settled, or permanent any more, least of all trees.

The sea laps my outside steps, and the crabs crawl up and patter among the dead gum leaves.

THE BUBBLE HOUSES are so common these days I no longer bother to count them. I used to sit for hours on the upstairs shadow deck, a little mechanical KouSeiki counter in hand, and click them off as they loomed out of the mist.

1187

1188

Sometimes I would see people leaning against the transparent sides. Some of them looked trapped, others relaxed tourists of the air. 1189 1190 1191

So: some of us are drifting away by water, and some by the currents of heaven.

THE MAIL-BLIMP ARRIVES for the last time. The head controlling it is not the usual elderly woman's, but one I know all too well. Every day in the mirror …

– I thought the crabs got you, I stammer (remembering the flaccid rolling corpse, remembering the temptation to try bacon of the unsalted kind (but that seemed to go too close the bone)).

– The crabs never got anything that counted, says Kei-Tu, and her smile promises revenge.

I take out a packet of Angus McNeil Seasmoke salmon slices, two phials of aromatic oils (Healtheries ylangylang, and venom), a quart jar of Vegemite (Sanitarium) and a sack of wild rice. I put in the last chapter of *The Neverending Novel*, and a mail redirection-order (so to speak), but I don't think the latter will work.

– Who is looking after your books? asks Kei-Tu. My library used to be famous.

– Any reader ...

– Where are you going?

– I don't know. Wherever the inward and ingoing tides take me. To stop temporarily wherever I strand.

Storytellers never stay in one place for long.

But I have spent too many words on my reply for the mail-blimp has already risen and floated away.

STANDING ON THE DECK of my home-made boat, I stare at the strange bolete. It had not shrivelled or decayed over the months, but extended hyphae through the rough little toetoe kete, and made the whole its mycelium. That is unnatural, hyphae being delicate and exceedingly vulnerable to changes in moisture or light – but what is natural now? I have seen a nest of shining cuckoos, and tresses growing from a skull ...

I had grown used to the basket-mycelium, grown used to the violent coloration. But now the fungus is glowing with minute blue sine waves moving up the stalk as the tide rises. It is the tide in microcosm, the whole cap becoming alight at slackwater.

I recognise a sign when I am given one so clearly.

I TAKE

the tide-bolete and the weather-clock

a blanket and a Swanndri and six silk shirts

a black iron kettle, a skillet and a griddle

a guitar and my favourite glass

the dictionaries – *OED* & Partridge for English, Williams, Tregear and Biggs for Māori, and Kraz for Chaotic: no other reference books. What I don't know now, I'll make up

sundry other things like food and drink and firing

myself.

ONCE UPON A TIME, we were a community *here*, ten households of people pottering through our days. We grumbled at taxes and sometimes complained about the weather. We cheered one another through the grey times, with bonfires and whisky and brisk massages. We sometimes sang when we were sad. We knew – the television told us, the radio mentioned it often – that the oceans would rise, the greenhouse effect would change the weather, and there could be rumblings and distortions along the crustal plates as Gaia adjusted to a different pressure of water. And we understood it to be one more ordinary change in the everlasting cycle of life.

Now, *here* is wherever you find me, and nowhere is where I'll be.

I AM BALANCED on the end bollard, the slip-rope in my hand.

There is one thing left to do before I jump aboard and drift away with my sulking trees.

I can't call this thing the *Hulmeship*: how about *Thumb-to-Nose*? Some great name from the past – *Sojourner Truth*? *The Stephen Hawking*? *Motoitoi Kahutia*? No: they are too great for a little boat whose only real freight is words. *Fish Dreaming*: now, that is poetic but I am afraid it isn't true. I wish it was.

The mists billow as land pulls away from sea, as another rift in reality occurs: a high-voiced flock of birds loops and twists round a passing stream of bubbles.

The *Pirate Epistle* enters your sphere.

Mushrooms and Other Bounty

Picking mushrooms, grumbling over their pale heads
sodden-gilled and heavy from continuing rain –

still, they are chance-fruit like frostfish
found on bitter glittering mornings

and the jewel phrases I have been given
by careless strangers, tossed over their shoulders;

and the real people who slid in from the black
at the back of my dreams and played

in naked brightness until
I imprisoned them in words –

chance-fruit: what past bones tuned my ear
to catch the inner chant of shining cuckoo song?

And once, walking a sea-line yet again,
I caught the only whitebait of that tide –
stranded by a sandbank in an errant finger of water
and already cooked by the sun –

A Deal Among the Makyrs

The gods of Literature o
those gods are not only
blind but caring and kindness
are not in their nature –

they toss promises into a deep crevasse
and feel, with feral curiosity, the splat
– or hurl them to far peaks
knowing that icicles and silence result –

they honk, they hoot, they spill the wine
while crouched around the great bronze bowl
playing their cards in a tangle of time.

The cards are strange and flattened people
grey and wenned, gouged and lined: they trust nothing
knowing they are trapped in the wordpool.

They struggle amongst the play, ineffectually.
Now and then one escapes into the wild light
of history

but when the gods yawn
and smile vacantly into a growing night
battered soiled cards are flopped down on a bone pile
– some whimper all heave a while but cannot unite
   fall silent

& the gods on their horny taloned feet
stagger away to their nests
arm in arm in arm
reeling through the dark, joking
in the swooping language
of the deaf –

The Pluperfect Pā-wā

WELL, I FOUND
that hyperbloodyinteresting, I tell you. *Fifteen* of them down on the beach and all of them out of their shells? Getting superbloodyconfident now, aren't they? And didn't I say that, right at the beginning? But no. Nobody listens to *me*. (You're captive, a captive listener. Reader. Whatever. You don't count.) (The interpolations – and this is mainly interpolation – are by me. You don't know me. You won't know me after this either. Don't worry about it. Just listen to him raving on about how we should have eaten them right away, instead of listening. What would you have done though? Me, I dropped the knife at the first squawk, and was *charmed*, right from 1's – do you put the apostrophe in for personal numbers? Not quite sure whether I was taught about this at school. Never mind, I was *charmed*, and I did what was asked, and I don't do that for all my fritters I assure you.)

Picture the new cathedral.

It is dense and made of bluegreen nacre: it is as fluid and ephemeral as a net of sounds: it is the holdfast rock (a volcanic dyke eroded to a halfmile stump but much more solid than the day it was born), and it is the unseen neural network, and it is the tides between.

Every ashtray made of Lucite with the chips in it; every

pendant, and cheap swinging earring, and dull stud in silver-plated ring; every 21st key; every napkin holder; every counter for housie; every salt and pepper shaker; every keyring; every designer necklace and silver work-of-art ring, swooping off your finger like a bird gone wrong, tangling in everything you touch; every flake ground into the gravel of path or beach; every haunted shell, in piles on the Stewart Island wharf, scattered the length and breadth of the islands (lengths, breadths) on beaches, in baches, in sedate suburban homes. Every last one of them. EVERY ONE.

(A bit of time goes by. Not more than a week. He's snoring off the effect of his after-lunch pubpet. I've just finished my after-lunch walk. Do you know, one of them said to me, quite shyly I thought, 'My first intra-generational mutation.' It was waving a chaplet of shining blue eyes, all loosely tethered to it by green filaments. The others (all sorts, I won't even try and describe them for you because the pace of change is getting hectic, and they're all experimenting madly) were giggling snidely at it. I said, 'Very nice. It seems nice and practical. It's beautiful. I like it. Nice.'

They're not talking much to me any more. They've given up on him altogether, but that won't come as a surprise to us. I *told* him it was Not A Good Idea to go and gut and eat sashimi-style that last ordinary he found. Don't tell him, but I saw his pubpet practising blowing bubbles just now. Isn't it *interesting* that never-animate things are catching it? Well, I suppose it was animate once, now you come to think of it. They're made of plastic after all, and plastic was once dinosaurs. I think. I know I learned something like that at school. Yes, that was it, layers of squashed animals and plants that turned into tar and oil and coal. So that would explain how a container for beer could link in. Wouldn't it?)

Speculation about the first one:
how did it discover itself as a thinking being?
how did it discover us, and our information hoards?
how did it learn to shape itself?
how did it pass on both knowledge and *ability* to accomplish these things to every other one?
Speculation about them all:
how did they discover the interconnection between life, the universe and everything?
And time and space?
Why won't they tell us?
Why are they ganging up on us?
Speculation is not a series of questions, though life ultimately turns out to be so. This is what happens to a philosopher in despair. Think about something else. Become the thought.

(SING! SINK DOWN SLOOWWLLEEEEEEEE … SING! SINK! SING! AHHHH! ROCK BOTTOM! THE WATER BREATHES ME AND WE BREATHE IT! WE BREATHE WE WREATHE WE WEAVE WE SIEVE WE ARE! SING! SING! NOW CLING! CLING! DON'T EVER LET THE ROCK GO! CLING!)

(I once had a nightmare about going down to my favourite mahika-kai for pāua. That was the beginning of the nightmare, and it seemed quite pleasant for a while, doing in a dream what I liked doing best of all awake, gathering food from the sea. I picked pāua – it was easy because there were dozens of them grazing the reef, ignoring me: they slipped off rock into my kit with never a clamp-down. I had a kit full in what seemed like seconds, though you can never be sure about time in dreams.

It was when I began to gut them back at the head of the beach that things turned nasty. Take out the fish, beat shit out of it on a handy rock, careful of the pewa, and then nick the radula out. All ready for steak, yum yum. But these pāua weren't ordinary inside: they were grey spongy stuff, which kept oozing out everywhere. I couldn't get it off my hands, even when I flung the kit away. I was screaming at the stuff, I never knew pāua had brains! I never knew!)

Casually say to yourself these three sentences;

one: everything that is, is interconnected;

two: everything you can think of, exists, and everything you can't think of, does too;

three: you are what you eat.

Now, go away and sort out which one, if any, was the lie.

(CLING!CLING!CLING!CLING!CLING!CLING!CLING!)

(Do you like millennialist fiction? You know, we have arrived at the crucial time for Humanity, and DOOM is upon us. The Norns have given up watering Yggdrasil. The Moirai have stopped all that weaving – it made a pretty pattern but never got *them* anywhere. Māui is abroad in our world once more, pretty pissed off at being kept out of things for so long, but ready to give us a whirl (chuckle). Things read very grimly, but you *know* that the author will sort things out at the end – one quirky brave couple of homo sapiens (homo sexuals if it's really post-modernist) will survive And The World Will Go On. I read millenniallist fiction because it's SO reassuring. Don't you find it so?)

Well, I found that fuckingbloodyannoying, I tell you. Well, I can't tell you. Yes I can. Someone will come along one of these days and we'll get together and get it together and by bloody hell, we won't make any mistakes next time round. We'll screw everything down so tight, NOTHING else will get a look in. Someone won't be the bloody useless wife, incidentally. *She* joined the early Sinkers, after running away with the pot plant. Said it had a longer bloody reach or something. Never did like the fucking thing, anyway.

Everything got impossible there for a while. Like, went down to the old piecart at the corner for a pie – not a real pie, the cattle had seen to that weeks before. Block-voted a veto along with the sheep and the pigs. Well, I don't really blame them, would've done the same bloody thing in their place, myself. Well, no, actually I fucking wouldn't. I'd've murdered us, the whole fucking lot. Nah, wasn't a real pie, it was goo – goo pie with goo peas on top, all you could get because the plants had gone berserk too. Made some comment about the weather and the thing behind the counter snarls Whaddarya? Fuckin' pāwāist or something? Didn't argue. Built like a bloody tank, and I mean really. Bloody great steel shell on it, and creepy 70 mm barrels peeping out under the black flesh fringe. Hey, better watch m'self, might go poetic like the fucking ex.

O well. After I got to Washington and found the button and set off everything from that end, I thought all would be well again. I waited in the mobile for a while – hell, I'm *proud* of myself for that mobile! It's got *every*thing, own atmosphere, foodmaker, and I could communicate with God if I wanted to. Thing'll give you booze, drugs, sort of sex, and it wasn't that hard to build. Kind of like I was the only brain left, being the only real man left, that I knew about, and everything we'd thought of before was mine. Built it a week after the wife sunk. Well anyway, aimed the fucking mobile home back to the beach. Might as well stick to what you know, eh? Thought I'd wait for the first decent looker to come along and we'd shack up and away we'd go, man on top again as it always was, and always should've been. But everything else in the world was charred. All the sheilas had either sunk or turned into something else or been so fucking dumb they hadn't built themselves a mobile. As I said, I found that extrabloodyannoying.

Never mind.

I can wait.

Something'll turn up.

It always fucking does.

like hollow hissing laughter
the cinders rustling
in the wind

(Oh no. Don't turn serious on me, not at this stage, not on this stage. Here, she says kindly, have this motto found in a Chinese fortune abalone. Look! It says,

PLUPERFECT (TENSE) EXPRESSING ACTION COMPLETED PRIOR TO SOME PAST POINT IN TIME SPECIFIED OR IMPLIED: PĀ (V.T/V.I/N) TOUCH, BE STRUCK, STRIKE, HOLD PERSONAL COMMUNICATION WITH, AFFECT, BE CONNECTED WITH, ASSAULT, OBSTRUCT, INHABITANTS OF A FORTIFIED PLACE, BLOW, REACH ONE'S EARS, GROUP, CLUMP, FLOCK: WĀ (V.IN) INTERVAL, REGION, DEFINITE SPACE, INDEFINITE UNENCLOSED COUNTRY, TIME, SEASON, BE FAR ADVANCED, CONDEMN, TAKE COUNSEL, SO-AND-SO

How neat to get that one! Much better than, say, THE WINDS OF CHANGE WILL SHORTLY BLOW THROUGH YOUR LIFE, or some such irrelevant guff. Much better to get that one, eh?

Have another fritter.)

Some Foods You Should Try Not To Encounter

The Anthropophagic Oyster

The anthropophagic oyster (=a/o) is immortal, blessed with incredible strength and speed, immune to heat and cold and anything sharp (or blunt), and very *very* angry about what had happened, is happening, and might happen – without its intervention – to its kin.

It is quite large, about 3x the size of your plumpest Bluff succulent, but looks just like any other oyster. Until it opens its eyes. It has two of them, a malevolent pale grey gaze with pinpoint black pupils.

It is quite disturbing to see them gleaming at you, with hate, from the centre of your plate, where it has been sheltering under a pile of delicacies.

It is much more disturbing to see its mouth open. It is nearly as wide as the a/o, and is filled with tiny but extremely sharp teeth. It has been known to slide down a gullet and eat you from the inside out. This is bad enough, but there can be a greater misfortune: anyone who has encountered the a/o among a nice presentation of, say, angels-on-horseback (I'll just leave that deliciously large one till the end, you tell yourself), or rearing out of a scrumptiously-thick perfectly-cooked oyster chowder and having the thing take a sizeable hunk off your lips or tongue, NEVER eats oysters again. Auē! Auē!

The False Lawyer's Wig

Next time a dinner guest deliquesces after eating your mixed-mushroom surprise, consider whether you may have gathered a False Lawyer's Wig by mistake. Unlike the true Lawyer's Wig (aka the Shaggy Ink Cap aka *Coprinus comatus*), the False Lawyer's Wig has no intention of dissolving itself. O no: it is a creature of much larger ambition. It holds itself in readiness – sometimes for years at a time – for that wonderful moment in its life when a human chances along tra la la little basket in one hand, 'shrooming on its mind, and doesn't notice the slightly phosphorescent tinge to its (admittedly rather charming) wig-en-déshabillé, and la la! plucks it.

The moment the thing has been admitted to the company of other mushrooms (who normally shun it), it begins producing huge numbers of specialised hyphae. Once these come into contact with human saliva, then it's all over Jack, bar the shouting (and there's generally quite a bit of that). The hyphae extend with astonishing rapidity into every cell of the body: they collapse the cell walls and turn the cell contents into a viscous foul-smelling dark-green slime.

Removing this from your carpet is difficult. Explaining what happened to the spouse/partner/significant other of the deceased is also difficult. Getting rid of the five billion little False Lawyer's Wigs which will soon appear ALL over your house, is impossible.

It appears that the False Lawyer's Wig was developed by a secret wing of the IRD – one assumes by mistake. The spores were handed on to Treasury in some desperate interdepartmental contradeal (one hesitates to even think about that). The False Lawyer's Wigs, through counsel, have intimated that the world is intended to be their oyster.

Rutabaga and tofu make, in the circumstances, acceptable substitutes for most fungi.

The Quiet Blue Chilli

In the more exotic food markets, you will sometimes encounter items that seem familiar but look … slightly different.

The quiet blue chilli is an example: it is sedate and reticent amongst its rowdy scarlet neighbours. It hides from the loud viridian charms of green chilli. It doesn't whistle or pout or draw attention to itself. It sometimes has shy little black blossoms attached to its modest stem.

You may be attracted, tempted to purchase such an interesting but demure vegetable: this one is not a skite, you say to yourself. This one does not thrust itself forward. This one will be content to blend in with whatever else I put in the salsa.

Be warned: the quiet blue chilli, any teensy part of the quiet blue chilli, any humble wee droplet thereof, will turn you into a fourteen-stone blister.

The Exophthalmic Pie

You are in a strange small town. You have been driving for five hours, and the heater packed a sad forty k back. You are cold, nay almost hypothermic, and you *need* food.

Hooray! Here is a smalltown tearooms, with a smalltown

piewarmer inside, and smalltown old-fashioned just-like-Mum-made pies inside that.

A word about pies: you CANNOT tell a pie by its cover. The pastry may be golden, flaky, crisp yet delicate leaves of perfectly-blended flour and shortening, baked to gourmet perfection. Even the underside of that pie may be less than sallow. The aroma coming from the pie-warmer makes you salivate? They do it with aerosol sprays, you know.

So, you cannot tell what the pie is going to be like from the outside. Lifting the lid before you buy is not regarded as couth. Lifting the lid after you buy can be a worse error, however. Is that really a tiny beak amidst the glue? The light must be turning the egg that wan shade of blue. What internal organ coils in quite such a vermiform curl? O no, it moved.

Itdidn'titdidn'titdidn't.

There's only one thing for it, given your urgent need for something warming, sustaining. Buy and munch, inside sight-unseen.

While your tastebuds scream and fight a valiant tho' hopeless rearguard action against what is scrambling past them, your bugged-out eyes glimpse the rigid faces of the smalltown tearooms' proprietors. And their wideopen unmoving wildly-sparkling eyes.

What Not To Chocolate Fondant

The following have been tried, but could not strictly be called total successes:

lamb's fry;

cucumber;

eggshells (even with eggs inside them);
snails (particularly those you neglected to steam first);
brains, raw or cooked (in fact, let's face it, despite the best intentions of Friends-of-Alliance 'Delight Your Palate' committee, no offal combines particularly well with melted chocolate);
karengo;
aphids (I have seen best friends stabbing one another with toothpicks as the argument over whose greenfly that is struggling there waxes hot);
and pine boletes (aka ceps, aka the penny bun, aka *Boletus edulis*). The eight-inch ones, especially, are death to light conversation.

Items such as lettuce, Farex, mutton fat and millipedes are borderline, depending on the genera of your guests.

The Extremely Pickled Onion

This hoon in onion guise will goose the sirloin and play boisterous footsie with the corned beef. And that's only the beginning.

As it/their debauch continues, expect nothing but trouble. Chunder over your carefully arranged cress, and maudlin weeping in the darker corners of the sliced bread.

It has even been known to fart in your cheese sandwich. Pre-farted cheese is the last thing we need in this day and age, really.

Wheebles, Quinges, and Codsballs

You have fallen into the cocktail circuit, or, save you, the round of literary do's. Chateau Supermarket is known to destroy intestinal lining faster than it can be formed, so unless you wish to be condemned to the artificial orange juice, you must partake of the nibbles.

These have sophisticated names but can be regarded as coming from these three basic groups:

WHEEBLES: have little wooden sticks through them. Combinations of meat & cheese, fruit & cheese, fish & cheese, vegetables & cheese, and cheese & cheese, are popular. Avoid anything that still seems to be moving.

QUINGES: always come on a background of some kind of farinaceous matter. Biscuit/toast/pastry/tacos/quiche – you know the kind of stuff, all of it made from recycled cardboard actually. What is draped limply on top depends on the host's budget. It will always fall off onto your white sea-island cotton shirt if it contains tomato sauce. Avoid quinges whose topsides seem to be burrowing into their bottomsides.

CODSBALLS: *very* occasionally you will come across the genuine article (with rather sad cod attached). Eat this kind by all means. They are delicious. But, with great regret, I have to tell you that most codsballs are little round brown crumbed things, somewhat irregularly shaped. If you are lucky the balls will have been formed by someone who washes their hands, and the cooking medium will be an edible oil. Inside every codsball, regardless of how imaginatively they are labelled, is a microwaved & sloppy concoction that will retain deathly heat until dawn. Avoid, if you treasure the lining of your mouth.

Sometimes I Dream I'm Driving

The steering-wheel is slim, with raised almost sculpted lines to assist my grip, and it always feels cold and hard beneath my fingers no matter how odd, how dangerous, the drive becomes, no matter how sweaty my palms turn. The steering-wheel is darkgrey in my dreams, although I cannot now remember what colour it really was. Maybe it was red, to match the red leather upholstery. Maybe it was black, to match the paintwork. Maybe it truly was darkgrey.

The roads unreel before me. I straddle three or four lanes with ease. Occasionally, with disconcerting naturalness and inevitability, the Snipe turns amoebic and fissions, and I am driving both vehicles happily along different and separating roads.

In this vehicle, the roads are straight and sealed, and despite the fact that road markings and signage, catseyes even, were not around during my childhood (and these dream-roads are riddled with them, are riddles from them), I know them, the straight, endlessly straight, bitumen roads that cross the Canterbury Plains heading south to Oamaru, the roads that lead to home.

Not Christchurch home, but my nana's place, where she always has bread drying in the oven so it turns crisp and more potent than ordinary bread, and when spread with butter (which never is hard, or melted to grease, merely perfect spreadable golden butter), becomes a sacrament of welcome to the travelling child, a sign she has arrived safely again. Nana's place has a scullery, made magic because she always kept her flour and sugar in cloth sacks in tin liners in the kauri flour-bin. The scullery is redolent of homemade soap and old lino. The scullery is quite often just over the backseat of the Snipe, somehow wedged in there before the boot. More often, Uncle Bill's shed is there, with the ton of coal in the corner coalbox, Grand-dad's anvils and vices (where I once tried setting off bullets by locking them in and hitting them with a hammer – they were only .22s fortunately, and, even more fortunately, I couldn't get them to explode, resorting in my frustration to asking for adult help in the matter. Which this time, indulged eldest child of a first generation although I was, I didn't get); all the gardening tools, the long-handled ones, are stacked in another corner, and best of all, Uncle Bill's gun-cupboard, with the evil knives we weren't allowed to use, the two shotguns and the .303, .308 and 9 mm beasts Bill used when hunting. A reassuring optional extra, the shed, for any vehicle, even for the Snipe which had haul-down armrests and pullout ashtrays and gasp wow a radio with buttons that would whisk you from one preset station to another that (snick) quick.

Whether the shed's in the back of the back, or the scullery, or just the passengers, doesn't seem to make much difference to the road-holding capacities of the Snipe. It's a big, heavy, black car, elegantly solid, and powerful in its way and time ('Same engine as a Commer truck,' said the Oamaru uncles, nodding to each other, 'plenty of grunt'. Well, I never drove the relevant Commer truck, just a Commer van many many years later, and it had as much grunt as your average moped as well as all the aerodynamics of a brick. I put it in a roadside ditch once, when trying to adjust a contact lens – ditch? Nah, it was a sort of runnel, about six inches down, but the Commer van squealed and puffed and ground its gears and snorted until I had to flag down a passing car to give us a tow. The car dragged us out with ease. It was a Honda Civic. I sold the Commer shortly afterwards, still beetroot with embarrassment (me, not it), to a person who liked puttering through life). Once, driving to the hill-hut in the Tigers, my mother put the Snipe into a mud rut that came three-quarters of the way up the hubcaps. The Snipe revved a bit, was chopped down a cog (as we said to each other) and solidly, powerfully, chewed its way through a hundred yards of rut onto the solid, where it gave a kind of elegant shudder and sailed on once more.

Yes, I drive on water often, particularly in the Super Snipe. Dream roads frequently edge into fogbound causeways over lakes. The road narrows to a charcoal wisp, the sides steam and the black water creeps onwards. I know there is a knob on the dash specifically for this kind of travel but my fingers have forgotten where it is and I keep pulling out the cigarette lighter instead. Not that it matters very much: tarseal or mud or lake, the Snipe keeps going. It is just that one of the kids in the back seat will always reach over and tap my shoulder and complain we're not going very fast. I know the errant knob on the dash increases our speed by reducing friction (the owner's manual in its leather binding is quite clear on this point, the words underlining themselves as I read them again) so, reach down and pull the knob and blast, there's the red coil of the lighter again. But look, the black water is expiring in fog, and the fog is rising over the dwarf mānuka groves that alternate with the concrete balustrading of the longest bridge in the southern hemisphere, the Rakaia Bridge, all nine-eighths of a mile of it.

That was a childhood mantra, a mile and an eighth long, not your common quarter or half but an eighth, the measurement to be chanted whenever we crossed the bridge in daylight, but only during daylight. I don't know why we didn't say it at night. Rakaia was close enough to Christchurch for us older kids to be awake, and we weren't expected to be quiet when we were awake. Indeed, if my parents began singing, we were encouraged to join in. It is one of my favourite memories of the endless journeys south, my mother and father harmonising together, singing because they loved to sing, John a light tenor, Mary a fine contralto, and the songs any songs that came into their heads, from 'Little Brown Jug' to 'Toora loora lai'.

I can't remember them singing in the Snipe. John bought the vehicle the year he died, 1958, and that year was a terrible one, my mother becoming deathly ill after a hysterectomy and, in consequence, us six kids being divided up round relations. We weren't used to being separated and although we frequently fought among ourselves (and violently on occasion – I can remember socking one of my brothers in the stomach so it first winded him and then made him vomit all over the red carpeted floor of the Snipe. For which *he* got told off, not having enough presence of mind (or air) to tell on me), we also loved one another dearly, and were used to being an intrinsic gang, just us, just family.

John had his Humber Super Snipe, a car he had coveted for many years, for mere months before his heart gave out, at forty-two. It made an interesting statement, next car after the hearse in his very long funeral cortége; a sleek symbol of decent wealth, the wealth of a man who began his working life as a carpenter, and painter and decorator, and wound up, by dint of his own hard work and considerable skills, President of the Working Men's Club and President of the Business Men's Association (at one and the same time), Justice of the Peace; owner of and partner in two New Brighton businesses; husband of a beautiful woman; father of many children; proud possessor of the Snipe. Well, it was roomy enough to carry all the floral tributes that couldn't fit in the hearse.

I never smell flowers on any dream drive. Frequently there *are* smells (which I am told is slightly unusual in dreams). The leather is sunwarmed, and that is a distinctive scent, as memorable as the rankness of old butts in the three ashtrays. Sometimes, it's warm sausage rolls, or the slightly sulphury reek of egg sandwiches. The Snipe transported so many picnics. Occasionally, one of the kids has puked. ('Wind the window down *first* next time!') The Snipe transported so many kids, entire wriggly basket-ball teams, a marching girls' troupe, my brother John's Scout pack, my sister Diane's St John's Cadets group … by the time my siblings were involved in those kinds of activities, I could drive them and their mates legally, and yet they aren't among the passengers that freight the long back seat. People I don't know come out of the scullery, and sit for a while on the red leather. Very few of them talk. I can see them clearly, for the rear vision mirror takes up most of the windscreen. I can hear them clearly too, because I almost never hear road noise inside the Snipe, even when I drive through the dark lakes, even when we spin in mad circles on gravel, even when the bullet hail breaks all the windows – we were in such a frightening hail-storm once, coming back from Oamaru. It chipped the windscreen and left tiny sinister dents on the bonnet.

And once, feeling an uncontrollable wobble as I took us round a shingly corner just past Templeton one night, I hit the brakes hard and sent the Snipe 180 degrees fast, facing us back to Christchurch on the wrong side of the road in a breath-robbing instant. My warrior mother let me drive another ten miles further on, in a quivering silence, my siblings having all come wideawake in the spinning second but wise enough not to even whimper.

Mary had begun to teach me to drive when I was twelve, the year after my father died, and by fourteen, I was regularly spelling her on the long drives south. I came to know, relatively early, the mesmerising power of a grey road unreeling before you, the mesmerising power of a rainy road glittering before you as far as your headlights could reach, the mesmerising power of a road you came to know intimately but which could always surprise.

A tractor pulling straight out in front from a paddock of stubble. I remember the stubble. I remember the nondescript reddybrown of the tractor. I remember the ache in my young and very strong legs as I put everything I had into pushing the brake through the floor. And the shrieking sound and the smell of brakedrum against wheel.

We never had an accident in the Snipe, and it was the family car for many years. It was the other vehicles that the crashes came in, the humble creeping little beasts like the Hillman Imp, or the Commer, or the Avenger, or the Trekka, putty-coloured cars and vans with vinyl seats and jerky floor-shift gears, things you'd never bother to hose down or lux out, let alone cut and wax.

Simonize: Turtle Wax. The Snipe's grill was heavy chrome, with a lot of slots. The bumper bars were fat. Everything could be polished to a glory of mirrors, distorting mirrors turning a delicate face into a wicked or woeful gargoyle, and my own heavy features to an unlikely Buddha-serenity.

You got the mirrors after a lot of rubbing with a rag smeared with gritty thick orangeybrown acrid gloop. (You got the gloop out from under your nails with difficulty.) There was extra pocket money as a reward for doing the car (as we said) provided you did a good job. We often pooled our energies. For instance, I preferred creating mirrors, but others like brushing out the interior (there was a good chance of coins being found in the smooth leather cracks) or cleaning the paintwork, because that was not only easy but even fun. There was a brush with long soft bristles, and a compartment in the handle wherein you could insert a pellet of special soap. The brush screwed onto a hose fitting – run the water, and presto! instant suds. One of my sisters became besotted with the bubbles so produced and sprayed away many months' worth of pellets. She was not popular. One of my brothers made himself even less popular by attempting to prove the boot of the Snipe was waterproof.

But it never leaks in the lakes of dreams. The coal is always dry in the shed, a little dust moting the air: my nana's flour is safe in the kauri bin, always ready to be made into bread to be made into a wayfarer's sacrament. The Snipe bowls along the long roads of the night, the wheel cool and hard and ready between my hands, and if the people on the back seat are quiet, why, sometimes they smile –

From Fisher In An Autumn Tide (bit 3)

bubbles …

from the winter-rusted willows
from the old bone in the shallows
from the watching shadow

that could be a fish:

eyes which look through unnatural windows
mistake the obvious, see hopeful matter where
there is no warrant

light strikes me so hard now.
An unwary glance see! sunlight
see! a match struck in the dark
see! torch flick
blinds, I see nothing except that obscuring flare
greenish overwhelming all the world out there

– one of my brothers says Don't you wish we could
wake up one morning
just *one* morning and *see*?

See around us?
See what waits?
See where we're going?

Yeah

We all have interesting feet in my family.
Our toes cringe as soon as we get out of bed.
They would sigh if they could.
Instead, with scarred & practised tentativity
they feel our way into the day:
groping is our mode of being
fingering guessing where the solid is listening
with myopes' too-sharp ears for the way.

I have tried to hear fish.
Wiser, today I flick a fly to the shadow by the trailing willow
split shot clips the water there is no splash

nothing happens.

A purist would say Kaitoa, good job, serve you right,
sneering the while at the little baitcaster, pistol-grip rod and
dinky svelte-profiled teardrop reel, sneering at the contemptible
2 k nylon, the kind that does not throw any reflection show
any kind of light; sneering at – but I tied that straggly black
spider myself, mate,

and underwater it must look like tucker because it's fooled
and killed
two fish to date –

that's all I'm doing today, pothunting not practising any high
form of
The Art, The Game, The Way.
I'm fishing for my stomach's sake and the keener for it.

To my mind, you're either playing – so, call it sport
(call it fishtorture as an animal-rights cousin of mine does if
you're so inclined;
that neither upsets nor enlightens me, having figured out early
there are 2 sides in every
game, whether you're a party on an ancient ball court or
having fun by yourself or
stumbling round life)
but you're basically playing or
you're there to catch food.

I'm here, having at shadows
which don't move.

Why has nobody invented a fishscope for us myopes?
Oh yes, I've tried binoculars. They make the indistinct
clearly indistinct, wobble the world alarmingly and magnify
sunglints
to sear so hard that's it for the day.

And as for anything else, polarised fishing-specs and things
– I'm the one wearing sunglasses to the bonfire
at midnight –

I need a fish-spotting device.
They used to call them cormorants, shags in our parlance,
equip them with a choker and retrieval-string and
send 'em out for lunch.

The shag on the stump over there
spreads its wings wider, and sneers.
The sunlight beams.
O well, I'll keep on fishing blind then

and a fin fingers
a fin fingers my line

Hours drift by before I realise they've evanesced.
Days so, years, and with them the might-have-beens
that died, that went beyond regret, returning only as hard memory
– I mean, solid, steely, pinching the mind suddenly
as this tool pinches the hook,
forceps relocated from a city A&E one tense evening – they clattered
on the floor and were ignored and I absently
picked them up from the fringe of things and toyed with them and

tucked them in a pocket.
How do you explain such petty forgetful theft? So
attached to a black reelup, pinned to my beltpouch, they no longer
clamp arteries, just hooks, tiny hooks, this hook I've defanged and now
slip out: she lies stunned still.
A hen trout: she had danced and fought up the riff of water
for twenty minutes sleek power in the dying sun
until drawn to the dubious safety of a net. She weighs
about three pounds I think but I've already killed a heavier jack
and she danced so well.
He'll feed the three of us – holding her gill-on to the current moving
her gently forward a little forward into the blind water.
Her fins flicker wearily, she weaves slowly off, but she doesn't bleed and
she'll do. I think, she'll do.
Live, that is.
There was a lot of blood that evening in the A&E, enough to make skilled fingers slippery
and instruments skate away. They should practise on fish maybe,
for the grip I mean. Then again, that's only if I want to hold to kill.
That hen, lost in the brown distance, felt wet cotton gloves but never suffered

pressure or the flame of my flesh – as for other
suffering, who can tell? I can't hear fish scream or
moan either.

The forceps tuck back against my belt.
Enough for this evening, I think.

The Eyes of the Moonfish See Moonfish Pain

SOMETIMES THE CATCH is a slab of dead bodies, blast frozen originally, now partially thawed. Dead bodies crushed by countless hundreds of their fellows, and by the time they come in, a little decayed.

The pick men go to work, hacking at the slab, spitting and swearing. Haw haw they laugh. She processes her pile. Scales fly and the grey matter from the guts runs over her plastic apron and seeps into her boots. She is meticulous about her head-cover, but the stench of the body slab seems to creep through the protective cloth. She feels her fine black hair turn stringy, then thicken somehow with adipocere.

The slabs are good for the pocket: a bonus is paid after you have processed a hundred kilo, and even with her arthritically-stiffening hands, she can through-put five times that.

Through-put?
Put through.
Her father juggles another
hot potato.

There had been a word – a phrase? – for that, too.

Every morning before there is light, she rises, washes herself in the tin bucket, and then uses that water to scrub the floor. The floor measures three feet by six feet, and is made of thin wooden planks. It is pallid now, from years of daily scrubbing.

Her fingers ache already: she ignores the pain.

Still in darkness, she folds her mattress in three and pushes it onto the wide waist-high shelf. The cotton-padded sleeping quilts, two of them in faded Chinese blue, go on top of the mattress. Then she sets the scrubbing brush, its bristles turned towards the coming sun, on the upturned bucket. She hangs her towel above it on the peg set in the side of the door, and the sacking apron at the end of the shelf.

She takes the clean inner gown and changes into it: the one she has slept in, her only other inner gown, she will wash tonight, and it will dry, nearly, in time for the following day. Her outer gown is made of coarse grey woollen material, shabby but clean. Her felt boots are also grey, many times resoled.

She uses the honey bucket, and then silently puts it outside the door. The sky is still dark.

At the far end of the tiny room is a charcoal brazier: she fans the embers to useful heat and waits, kneeling, her hands folded in her lap, until the kettle boils. Why were we called the long bright land? she wonders. She can hear her father's voice quite clearly: 'Aotearoa? O, it means the long bright land. Where did you get that old book?' The voice is clear, but she can no longer remember her reply, nor where the book came from, nor what it had been about.

She drinks a cup of kombu-cha, and eats a bowl of packet noodles. It is time to go to work.

◆

The factory is huge: it has concrete floors, and half walls, and the roof – a hundred metres above her head – is made of Polylucite held up by bare steel girders. She has never learned exactly how large it is, for a maze of cutting benches and wash areas, managerial cubicles and processing tables and free-standing blast-freeze chambers has grown over the years since she began to work here. When she had first timidly entered the side-door labelled WORKERS, there were already many little rooms scattered over the vast floor, and the distant walls were partially concealed by lean-tos and platform floors, strange machinery and shadows.

She goes quickly to her assigned work area on the west door side. The leading hand looks at her: the gaze shows neither approval nor disapproval, because she is only seven minutes early, the period of median grace, not early enough to indicate exceptional eagerness, not too close to starting time, and so hinting at dissatisfaction or rebelliousness.

She picks up the knives, and runs a stone over each sharp edge, polishes each already gleaming blade. She is deft and fast enough to make the rank of Able Hand first class, but she chooses to hide her speed, her skill. Outstanding nails get hammered down,

says her father,

tall poppies get chopped.

Some days, it is just dead things; some days it is frozen dead things. Today, they are live. A great ship is drawn up to the main wharf at the far distant east end, and the first conveyor belts are nosing into her holds. All too soon a subsidiary conveyor is stationed in front of her working bench. The belt whines, and begins to move towards her, an ever-steady creeping of one metre every thirty seconds. She holds her iki-pick ready, ready for anything – long eel pouts, phosphorescent crabs, stocky-bodied boxfish, a swarm of pioke still thrashing as the cleats drag them out of the live-box the conveyor has towed behind itself to here.

She knows the place for crustaceans, the place for boney fish of small size or large, the place for primitive fish. She daggers the iki-pick in exactly. If her workmates notice her for anything it is the fact that she kills large and small items equally well, a two metre pioke or a ten centimetre paddle-crab chik! dead.

She never thinks of anything while eating lunch. The fish stew, with steamed quinoa in a separate bowl, is tasty enough, and you can buy additional relishes – shoyu and ginger, or crushed garlic in shichimi togarashi-flavoured oil. On the three feastdays of the year, the Wheat-Golden provide rice, steaming sticky mounds of it, and the tart low beer almost everyone else seems to enjoy. She never buys a relish: she sips less than half a mug of low beer, eats but one bowl of rice, on the feastdays. Moss, who works next to her, asked her once, 'Are you supporting elderly kin?' Moss is a loud and bawdy woman, with strange pasty skin white as the bean buns of the New Year. The question is as intrusive as ever a question will get in these times. She had raised an eyebrow, and half-smiled. Moss blurted, 'I know you live in the Summer Gardens, so it is not a matter of, it is not.' She blushed to the roots of her mud-coloured hair. It is not a matter of paying most of your wage to live in a respectable, a comfortable, area. She said – gently, because Moss had once given her a pottle of fishbird oil to massage into her arthritic hands – 'I do have commitments. I enjoy what there is available here. I feel no need for further spices and flavourings.' I am lucky, she had added, and Moss had smiled in relief.

Today, Moss is working opposite her. The pasty face is rigid against the pain movement causes her. A weeping pink rash shows above her collar. Fishhandler's disease, erysipeloid of Rosenbach: she has read all the warning signs. She wears the flimsy gloves provided, and avoids spines and jabbers as much as possible. There is also red feed dermatitis, which comes with the summer mackerel, and she once watched a worker a belt away look in surprise as a tiny cephalopod scrambled away from his hand. The creature was less than five centimetres long, initially a dirty yellowish-brown in colour – except now there were brilliant turquoise striations on its body as it sought shelter under another pile of fish.

The worker had vomited a little later. His speech was thick as he tried to explain why. Within half an hour, they had tugged him to one side, and laid a fish-crate cover over him. His breathing had been stertorous and hard before he died.

In the Summer Gardens, locks are necessary. If you have an elaborate lock, someone will soon notice, and wonder what you have that is worth the lock. If you have no lock, someone will soon notice, and rifle the little you have. She has a discreet palm plate, and a steel-framed door. She is known in the area. It is known she has very little, and does not earn a lot.

The lock is sufficient.

The door opens at her hand's touch. She slips inside, and closes the door, noiselessly. She takes her boots off, and kneels down by them a moment.

There is the immaculate metre of scrubbed wood floor: there is the worn but golden metre of sleeping tatami. Both stretch ahead of her for six feet.

A yard, a yard, said her father,
our masters give us a yard for sleeping
our masters give us a yard for walking,
how generous our masters are!
His twisted face so bitter.

She stays a moment more on the foot-wide strip of coir-matting, a guard against street soil. She stares at her far wall, another foot-wide strip, the last foot-wide strip. The brazier on its firebricks: by it, the kettle and double-steamer pot; on the shelf above it, the box of noodles, the jar of kombu-cha, and the old gourd, with the odd looping curved incisions on it, that holds the only seasoning she uses; a tea-bowl, and a noodle-bowl, a porcelain spoon and a pair of eating sticks with ancient ivory handles, propped upon their rest.

◆

Her bedding, and spare gown, and the bucket and brush … o, and the roof window which lets in a square metre of light on very fine days. She smiles grimly to herself. Yes, the palm lock is enough, it seems.

And we did own all the islands,
said her father as he died.

She knows only this part of this city. And one place else.

She washes carefully, filling the bucket twice from the communal tap, once for her body and once for her hair. She puts on the fresh undergown, and washes the one she has worn. Then, because it is the monthly payment day, she goes out to the tiny corner supplies shop that serves her block. She replenishes her noodle and kombu-cha containers, sufficient for another month. As always, Mrs Nehu-san bows, and gives her a tiny gift. She bows deeply in return. Once, Mrs Nehu-san had said, 'Your skin is a lovely colour, almost that of a Wheat Golden.' She had smiled properly, and bowed properly in return for the compliment. Mrs Nehu's skin is brown, although they both share the same wavy darkbrown hair, and brown rounded eyes, and solid short-legged bodies.

Their women used to be bandy-legged
said her father,
from all that kneeling down, but don't
remember that.

Safely back inside her austere room, she replaces noodle and tea containers, removes her other grey gown and hangs it up.

Now is the moment of the month: now is the reason for continuing to be.

She is relaxed, at ease, an obvious habitué of this place. Her head and the top part of her face are hidden by the elegant silk folds of a shadow hood, but her hands are slender, the nails short and lightly-oiled.

One of the old class, he thinks, no implanted diamonds for *them*. The kimono she is wearing backs up his thought. It is made of heavy lustrous grey silk, with occasional random fernshapes in silver. Definitely one of the first civilising groups – they tended to use the old motifs to show a kind of casual empathy with those-before.

The servitor clearly knows her: he has brought a menu, but doesn't show it to her, whispering earnestly and discreetly into her shadow-draped ear. Her answer is low, beyond audibility, but the servitor bows promptly and respectfully and hastens away.

Bit of a mystery, he thinks. Know many of the first-civilisers in this smog-ridden plains city … a Honshu-san? Their women were known to venture into this water world. But she seems too tall for a Honshu, and besides they will shamelessly drag along an entourage, and be bare-faced to boot. One of the Kandaisu-sans? Now, they're *old* class, came for the jade originally, and now have got it all sewn up,

and, as if in confirmation, sees,

as she leans to delicately reposition the steaming cup, the beautiful shell, the balanced green shreds on their plank,

the jade piece on the heavy silken cord around her neck.

He beckons the servitor, and carefully tucks a hundred-tara note under his soup bowl. He says, 'I am a connoisseur of old pieces of jade. I should like to discuss this small love of mine with the person who sat opposite me, the lady in the shadow hood. Is this possible?'

The servitor's face is bent. He does not show distaste, he does not show interest. He has already noted that this yakuza's attendant slipped out after the Woman Who Eats at the End of the Month. 'All things are possible, honoured sir. I will enquire further.' He has no intention of doing that. The yakuza is a passer-through: The Woman has been coming here for twenty years.

'You do not know her?' The voice is quiet but edged.

'She chooses to remain known to herself. She comes here regularly, has done for many many years,' and wonders whether he has just heard that strange low far-off cry.

She has put the three-fold mattress onto the scrubbed wood: she sits upon its grey scrim cover and looks into the hole. It is not large, this hole. Her father had pecked it out on the rubble that makes the base of her room. He had taken nearly a year to accomplish the hole, and obtain the linings for it, and inscribe the verse beside it. Her father says

Ko Aoraki te mauka:
that means realm of heaven is
the mount,
ko Waitaki te awa,
the river of tears is the way,
ko *Takitimu* te waka,
the vessel is *Takitimu*, I do not know
what the name is, and
ko Kaitahu te iwi, the beloved people
are the people, says her father,
and I will just write my real name here
for you, and he dies.

I know how to live, she tells herself silently. She takes off the heavy silk kimono and lays it in the scented wooden chest. She places the shadow hood on top of it, and the little woven basket that contains the nail oil, the hair dressing, and the few remaining drops of body scent. Reluctantly, and with great care, she takes off her mother and lays her on the silk. A swathe of silk on top of all, the lid of the chest closed, the rough mat on top of the lid, the black plastic carefully enclosing it, the thin slab that looks just like the rest of the concrete under the sleeping tatami on top, and then she lays the tatami down.

'Sweet dreams,' she whispers to her hidden mother, her gone father, her quiet and satiate self.

Her mother floats in the air before her. She is singing very softly, Kāti tō pōuri rā, hine e hine.

Her mother is a hundred millimetres tall and eighty

millimetres wide and she is heavy for her size. Her eyes gleam in a startling way, for they are made of pinkish abalone shell, but the gleam is that of gentle vitality, and does not terrify. Three of her fingers rest on one curved token of thigh, while the other three gesture towards her open mouth. She is a beautiful translucent green, with grey and blue mingling in the green. She resonates with compassion and power.

She is famous in her time,
says her father with quiet pride.

The singing fades. The water-glow dies. The night grows.

As she waits for the water to boil, in the dark before dawn, she relives the meal.

The scallops arranged in the spider lambis were succulently decadent. A bottle of rare wine had been reduced to its essence and sprinkled over the raw bodies, and rough salt, and finely-chopped redware. The flush of the shell echoed visually the wine and the seaweed, and although there were but five scallops, they were truly sweet meat. The slices of mild green pepper were almost transparent, and they tangled artfully with shreds of young daikon, and pressure-steamed fragments of tī. Hot and crisp and oily-melting, a challenging blend. And the tea, as always, was Black Dragon tea, a hint of smoky coolness in the steam, and a consummation in the mouth. People died just to get it to these islands she had learned.

She could think of many worse reasons to die.

The scallops cost four days' work each. The salad cost two days'. The cup of tea was the usual six days', and the gratuity, a large part of the month's bonus.

This coming month, they may have crabs in berry. Two would be enough.

On the mornings after, she drinks a single bowl of hot water. The last swallow has gone down. It is time to go to work.

A thousand thousand blue cod.

Frozen slabs of ghostly deepwater fish.

A surprise of lively squid slipping off the conveyor belt and flaring their hoods, ruinously squirting jets of stinking black ink over all comers.

Eels and eels and eels and eels.

The days are only fish, to be scaled and filleted or sliced, to be killed and sorted and gutted. Some early mornings she cannot remember what work she did the day before. Who cares?

says her father,
Who cares what the day brings?
The night will always come.

·

There were four days of no work available, when she sat in the sun with the rest of the west-door workers, but there was an equivalent in bonuses. Twenty-six days' pay, and her small emergency hoard. It will be enough.

There was only one crab in berry, but nearly as large as her two spread hands. The breathing organs had been removed, and the hopeful pod of ochre-red eggs sprinkled artistically over the exposed white flesh. She ordered two chicons with a salt wine dressing, and because they were very cheap (chicons are only dear in spring), had dancing shrimp broth as well as the tea.

She is absorbed in the slow curling and straightening of the dying crustaceans when a polite but burr-edged voice says,

'Forgive this unseemly intrusion, lady of the shadow hood. I am called abruptly away from this floating-world, but need to tell you that the unexpected gift is always the most appreciated.'

He bows, his forehead near to the restaurant tatami. The tattoos that curl brazenly over the back of his neck tell her immediately what he is. He stands quickly, bows once again, briefly, and strides away. His three dark-kimono'd attendants slip anonymously after him. They do not look at her.

She has gone to her knees in front of the door. It is an inch ajar. She can see, through a numbing fog, the laser-drill holes round the palm-plate, and the raw gouges in the steel frame from a torque-jemmy.

There had been an afternoon an age ago, a year ago, yesterday, when the progression of conveyors came to an abrupt halt. A stir of managers emerged from their private rooms, and all around, the hands laid down their picks and knives. She had quietly completed the things that lay upon her stopped conveyor belt, while Moss craned and peered to see what the matter was. 'Oh poor thing,' she said. 'Poor thing.'

She had looked up then.

Three managers are fussing about a huge fish on a trolley. They are personally adjusting gauze and pressure bubbles about the fish, which is quivering. It is beautiful, she thinks, for a fish. Dark-blue on its back, and purple and gold on its flanks, and a vivid scarlet on the belly and fins and jaws. Overall, joining the bright slashes of colour, is a scattering of irregular silver spots.

'What is it?' she asks the leading hand diffidently, softly so the organiser can not hear her if he chooses.

'Live sashimi.' He grunts. 'An opah, a moonfish.' The red fins quiver. 'The highest of the high will pay fortunes to eat it, very soon.' The great silver eye that is uppermost rolls a little. The trolley is ceremoniously pushed on. The conveyors begin again.

Moss said again at the lunch break, 'That poor thing. You could see its fear, you could feel –'

'It was only a fish.'

It is a long long time before she goes inside her door.

Hinekaro Goes on a Picnic and Blows Up Another Obelisk

SHE IS FISHING with spiders.

Not the fly kind: real spiders buzzing angrily inside a tangle of muka and web that makes a treacherous bob. Sooner or later, an eel is lured by the vibrating of anger, by the edible hope of the thing, to snarl its teeth in the tangle.

A gentle flick of the short stick – good, she's got that right at last – and the spider-bob is repositioned. There is the upward swirl, the light ripple, and the bob is taken. Carefully, carefully, draw it to the bank, smooth now, smoothly – o damn.

She notes the departing flurry of eel and spiders; the bony mud-splotched knees with scabs on each; the child's bleak disappointment, and then she's gone.

The knees are plump and ivory-coloured, and they are drawn to just under her nose. The floor is polished and greasy with her own sweat and other exudations, but in the corners are quivering piles of fluff and dust, slut-balls, tumblefuzz. Her hip aches. A moment ago the door creaked. The window knocked. She wraps a hand over her mouth and nose, don't sneeze, if you're quiet they won't look under the bed and you're safe quite safe –

The leg-warmers are striped lime-green and incandescent pink, are rumpled round the ankles and tight below the knees.

The hands are strong, with long brown fingers and well-kept nails delicately painted. Flush. The predominant feeling is outraged nausea.

– The dog! The filthy thing!

The lid is always down. There's never paper in the water. Sometimes there's just water …

– I'll, I'll

do nothing. Because this is the man who coldly threatened her dismissal when she left a note complaining about the porn photos under his desk blotter. This is the Money Bags and she's had enough of half-living on the dole.

Shit, pressing the button and cleaning the bowl. Under the seat. The cistern cover.

today be finnimbrunnous
eat savoury seameal custard sprinkled with crumbled black arame, and thin slices of smoked kahawai
plant a cinquefoil
fish for Flower-of-the-Wave
think: where do words go after the sound of them has died?

Hinekaro says,

'What don't you believe? Finnimbrunnosity? Catching eels with spiders and webs?' No no no, I say impatiently, I've done that myself, often. I can look that word up somewhere. It's this bit about a grown man leaving his shit deliberately unflushed … he's a high-powered executive for god's sake, why would he bother tormenting one of the cleaning staff in such a dirty-little-boy way?

Hinekaro says,

'You tell me, I can't get into their minds. A lot of them do it though, all levels of management, all levels of workers. And don't wipe their bums. Ask their mums. Their wives. Their daughters.'

I can't believe it, I say again. No way. And why doesn't she just flush the loo without looking, regardless of whether he's left the seat up or down? She's abetting her own victimisation, there.

Hinekaro says,

'Mmmmm. A point. I'll slip it in next time. I've got something better in mind though. Something more active, more my style.'

I wince. I've seen samples already of Hinekaro's style.

today be geely   be geeliouser

eat perfectly cleaned, non-membraneous December kina roes, with shredded lettuce and mango, and potato-yeasted potato bread on the side
plant a plantation of puapuatai
fish for stargazers with size 22 coch-y-bondhus
think: I have just written lies.
They are real lies.
They are true lies.

She gathers herself together, compacted and cold and

slimey. It had taken a bit of gathering too, but now it is done. She lurks round the bend, waiting. And as soon as his sphincter opens, she charges back upwards, and his shriek is overwhelmed by her shrieks of laughter, at least in her own ears. He'll be impacted for days, she giggles, and his attempted explanations will be choice. But to hell with them, she thinks, and hangs round, a waver of heat lines above the heating duct until Legwarmers comes in.

And while the cleaner never looks, for ever after she cleans a perfectly clean toilet. In that office anyway.

Under the bed the old woman is breathing hasty shallow breaths. The ache in her hip has spread to her chest, and the dustballs are soughing in her throat. The bang on the door is frighteningly loud, *real* and loud, and she clenches her eyes painfully tight, don't do that again don't *bang* don't come in *bang* don't and then the splintering sound, right behind her eyes.

It is quiet, and nearly dark. She can hear oystercatchers fossicking the incoming tide, and the sweet shy song of a cricket, zhirrit zhirrit, behind her.

She has stripped more flax for the muka, and new lines; she has found more webs and more spiders, and she has lost two more bobs. This has to be the last one for tonight (flick the line gently) because there's no moon around and she can't really see. But she feels the bob mouthed, nudged, and then nipped, and slowly she draws the line shorewards. The lack of light is doing strange things to her fingers: they look bigger and browner than usual, with lean ridges of muscle she hasn't got. The voice in her head says, 'Slow but steady, and when he's landed, just past your feet there, after this twitch, there's a stone with one sharp edge I chipped 200 years ago, so hit his head hard, just the once will do,' and she jerks too fast. The spiderbob rips loose, and her fingers are her own again, and the voice in her head (if it was a voice) says, 'Hmmm.'

today be owlerfied
eat the grilled crisped paperthin golden skin of a mutton bird, and steamed pūhā, and wedges of baked kūmara with coriander butter (nothing of these component foods to touch each other, except in the mouth)
plant a baobab
fish for raparapa
think: digesting the meaning of a word

Hinekaro says,

'I know you have an immediate interest, but telling you the possibilities won't help all that much. You can dream most of them up yourself.'

Well, that old lady for instance, what will she do? I ask.

Hinekaro says,

'I don't know. She could decide to come back immediately. Or she might want to hang round waiting until that young thug who knocked her over and stole her purse and came creeping and prying round her flat is frail and decrepit and threatened. Then she could snuggle in his remnant of mind and enjoy his terrors. An utu of a kind, enjoyed by many victims.'

Or? I suggest.

Hinekaro says,

'Some fade out of my ken, away from here, very quickly. There is an overpowering golden hole one way, an overpowering grey hole diametrically opposite, and you can see thousands of them flit either way, moths to candle and anti-candle, every minute. Then there are those of us who like to … be part of things.'

Part of things, I say after her.

Hinekaro says,

'Consider the bird-shit caterpillar.'

I beg your pardon? and I am genuinely bewildered.

'It has been noted for a century and more that there is a huge preponderance of beetles over all other forms of known life. That's because beetles are dead easy, quite a rigid ground plan of design. It's merely a matter of finding or inventing a niche nobody else has thought of, or a colour scheme, or wing arrangement that's slightly different. Presto! that's your initiating job done, and you can join in the network and be part of everything that ever there was and is and will be, world with an end amen. Shows a lack of imagination *I* think.'

But Darwin and Stephen Jay Gould? I sputter with indignation. Foster and Arapo and

'Te mea, te mea, te mea,' says Hinekaro. 'Consider the bird-shit caterpillar, a specialist in survival amongst moth offspring, and a fine piece of imaginative work if I may say so. In its early stages it uses disruptive patterning, and stiffly imitates twigs. The major crypsis is wondrous – but inexplicable if you're over there. I quote an entomologist you're familiar with, because his book is on your shelf there, and I've read it from the inside out: when the caterpillar reaches maturity (for a caterpillar, you understand, and you might like to consider that it still must pupate, and emerge to its final form), and becomes alarmed, it will

> 'curl up, the whitish parts of the first and the last segments visible, and the darker parts of the body in a whorl, so that they look exactly like bird droppings.'

You care to explain how the little beast evolved such a survival strategy?'

I'm thumbing through *New Zealand Insects and their Story* by Richard Sharell, and yep, there's the pictures of the larvae of *Declana egregia*, and the quote. And no, I don't want to attempt any explanation of how, eventually, random mutations achieve a patterning that looks exactly like a bird's dropping *only* when the caterpillar coils itself up.

I can't believe that, I say. Not that we have any input. We can – shape things.

Hinekaro says,

'There's an old saying: The more you look, the more you see. It is a misquotation. It should be, The more you look, the more there is to see.'

Well, I tuck it away, a future referent, and return to my original question, the one I put to her before you came in.

How long do I really have? I ask.

Hinekaro says,

'Just a minute – '

and flits away a bird without any shadow passing over head.

today be umber
  eat water
  plant rumours
  fish for kraken
  think: a whisper dies on her lips

The girl has come to the estuary edge just after dawn. I don't know why I'm doing this, she grumbles to herself. I've got dozens of eels, hundreds of them, hook and net and spear. But she does know why: to catch a fish with gear you can make from a bush and a clump of flax, and if you catch something, can cook in a small trench of heated embers, wrapped round in leaves. She's got the matches, but knows how to focus a magnifying glass, or use kaikōmako and māhoe for that matter. It's being independent of what other people have made for her; it is being self-reliant. What is self-reliant? she thinks suddenly. I don't know those words, and all the while her knowledgeable hands have felt the eel's touch on the spider and are drawing it calmly, inevitably, to ground writhing at her feet. And in the now-bright sunshine a daylight owl hoots softly, and flits over her head away.

Do you know how many years it has taken me to remember that? I ask.

Hinekaro says,

'Just tonight.'

You grow jaded, she said to me, as she waxed and waned in terrifying shadowiness, now a luminosity without definition that filled my room, now a pinpoint of intense dark. Her voice wasn't terrifying; it could almost have been my own.

I was a girl, she said, then I was a log. I was a log for generations, and they loved and feared me, a good omen for some of them, death for others. Then I spread further afield, the people spread further afield, and I quickened with the surprises, the newfound tastes and intrigues and ploys in the game of fish and fishing. I quickened with ripe hard-held hates … you may have an urge to revenge yourself? A food I haven't tasted? A new quality or not-yet-thing to be?

Well, I think, lying back almost comfortably into the dark, take three backsteaks from a yearling deer, fed on new-sprung bushtucker all its life. A clean-shot yearling, taken while gazing blankly away from you, a half-chewed leaf still in its mouth. And the marinade is two cups of the MacAllan and half a cup of cranberry jelly, ten cloves of garlic finely chopped, and two minced sage leaves, and soy sauce to your taste of salt –

'Yes yes,' says Hinekaro, smacking her – lips,

and after marinating it for an hour, you stew it gently, marinade and all the diced backsteaks, for two, and add a little cornflour and some rocksalt if needed, and let it cool. It is very good hot, but if you have a large cold bowl full of it, and some creamy oatcakes cooked on a girdle, and a salad of very young broad beans –

'Yes?' says Hinekaro

that's the beginnings of an outdoor feast. And there's that bloody monument to Sir Somebody, DDT, stuck up on the park hill, I could be a concrete virus or an earthquake-generated subsonic or even an unimaginative lightning-bolt –

'Yes,' says Hinekaro

invent fanged kitefish from those filmy things mutating off Mururoa, plant sundews and li-po, be umbelliferous, be lymphy, be sachemlike.

'Yes!' and I haven't even started on the fishing.

When you aren't reading these words,
says Hinekaro,
they turn into spoken Māori and roam wild.
Watch this space.
Watch this space.

Getting It

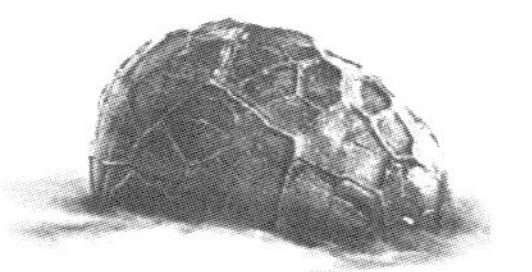

BORING

BORING

BORING

So far, we've had the concerned conservationist, a wet-eyed woman of mature years:

'In summation, I *beg* of you to take these cohabitants of our lovely coast, each of them as valuable as you or I'

– Councillor McMurtry rolls her eyes and snorts –

'in their own way of course, but valuable, please take them into account.'

At least she was concerned about spiders, a pleasant change from the usual birds or trees.

Then, the dour owner of a neighbouring property, sandalwearing yes, but looking as though he'd sooner eat spiders than save them. *He's* upset at the prospect of lots of trucks and noise and inconvenience to himself and noise and increased rates probably and noise.

'He's had the noise control officer out seven times so far this year. Last time it was about dogs barking. The farm was three k distant.' Sam's whisper is as engaging as everything else about her. 'Ooops, got to brief the next lot.' She tiptoes away.

Now we've got the local iwi rep rabbiting on about spiritual importance and cultural insensitivity and a violation of manawhenua blah blah te mea te mea. When I went to school with him, he was Paddy O'Shea and he used be rude to my gran behind her back (she'd've cracked him one with her stick if he'd been rude to her face.) Now he's Te Paringa Auhei and he had the cheek to ask me just before the meeting began, 'Did your lovely old tāua leave any whakapapa books or things like that e hoa?' He still understands a playground snarl.

Now he's doing a chant and stumbling over some of the words. Giving the hearing his best shot I suppose, but two of the councillors are murmuring together and anyway, everyone knows this hearing is a total waste of time.

Because the council has already decided that a subdivision – 'a boutique tasteful ecofriendly village' is how the developer's pamphlet puts it – a subdivision on the Neck is A Good Idea. More rates for one thing: more work for local builders and roading contractors for another, and more jobs for the large pool of jobless. Win-win for everyone, and besides, the land was going to waste. If Soamy Reischek hadn't been smart enough to realise it was unclaimed Crown land of no interest to Ngāi Tahu or DoC and so up for grabs, it'd just sit there, idle, useless except for breeding sandflies. O, and spiders –

so, boring.

Not that I'm unsympathetic to the concerns being expressed: it's just that, after ten years working round councils and such, I know how the system works.

The council's decision is a foregone conclusion and nobody's interested in objectors. One of the councillors has slumped sideways, asleep rather than dead, I think. The Mayor has his forehead resting on steepled hands. Soamy and his sharky-looking lawyer are smirking at each other. The council general manager and his secretary are whispering, totally ignoring Pat. Councillor Mooch is picking his nose in an absent-minded way. Someone really should tell him that's how the rest of his brain went west.

'Tihei mau reee ora!' declaims Pat.

'Ah. Thank you ah, Mr ah,' says the Mayor. 'And next ah?'

'I'm not quite finished your worship.'

'Ah.'

'You won't believe what's next!' whispers Sam excitedly and her delicious lips tickle my lobe.

I look at the order list and groan. Quietly.

The spider lady; the man with tender ears; Paddy. The elderly hippy clan who were next had been effectively sidelined by the council cruelly holding the hearing on the day before benefit day. So it has be the nut group next. I had already labelled them The Flax Leaf Scribblers. Imagine making your objection to a proposed subdivision on a flax leaf – way to be taken *really* seriously eh? Pissed the hell out of the photocopy clerk I can tell you. Still, it made a nice paragraph ('Committed conservationist recyclers should take note' etc.) and I admit the printing was very neat.

We're already an hour over normal sitting time.

And I've got to write up this dreck afterwards.

For crysake put a sock in it Paddy.

But he goes on translating, sort of, what he's already said, 'and if you wound our mother, she will fight back. She will destroy you, yes indeed. Death will take you, yes, that's true. Yes! Yes! Kss kss hei. There isn't really a translation for that.'

'Ah. Thank you. Thank you.'

Paddy doesn't look at me as he pushes out the big double swinging door. Figures I've sold out probably.

There is a short pause. People rustle papers, slump further sideways. Then the doors creak inwards.

Hello, that's interesting: it was cold and raining hard when I entered the meeting. Now it seems to have turned to fog. Little wispy tendrils float into the room.

Sam, standing in front of the council table, announces,

'Speaking to their submission, objecting to the proposed subdivision, ur Te Hā o Neherā.'

Lemme guess, Ancient Nation of Waita freaks. Or maybe

SHIT!

He stands about two and a half metres tall and he's covered in long red hair. It drapes down his belly sort of covering his sex. He stinks, rancid meat and freshcut fern and something like ancient sweat.

She is only slightly shorter, and is possibly hairier: she has tied little shells to her belly fur and they hang down right to there and clink and clitter as she lumbers across to stand by the male, facing the Mayor and council.

Whose collective jaw has dropped.

The things stare around with huge black mournful eyes.

I note the male is clutching a long bone, with holes drilled in it. It looks unhealthily like a femur.

Fresh primate femur. Which fact goes whizzing round in

my brain so hard I don't notice the entrance of the next two – beings.

One is a little horror, hairless, face pale as foam under moonlight, with eyes that are wholly red. No pupils, no whites. Its nails are red too, bloodred on hands and feet, but any other strangeness is hidden under a wrapping of cloak. A cloak that looks to be made from thick cream twilled silk.

It's best muka, retted and beaten to silken smoothness, such as I have only seen in museums.

And, moving to head the little company is –

o dear, I remember far too many of Gran's stories, and there's only one thing this could be.

Slender and elegant with hair like toetoe in the sun, and large deeply green eyes – imagine almondshaped lenses of clear kawakawa poenamu come very much alive – those kind of eyes.

Dressed in a black kneelength rāpaki, but not like any rāpaki I've ever come across (Gran was the last weaver who made them: they look odd but are surprisingly warm and comfortable. There's a soft loose-weave lining, and many layers of rolled end-knotted strings which sway as you walk. I've never felt so lithe and sexy as when walking in a rāpaki.) But *this* rāpaki has little green beetles flying out and around at erratic intervals, tethered on invisible threads. A tiny clematis vine is growing around the waistband. Naturally, it's in full flower. And for a top, the being has a kind of bolero made from kākāpō feathers, soft and gorgeous mottled mossgreen feathers.

Only they move. A subtle lifting, shifting, resettling –

while the tūrehu stands perfectly still on its bare feet, luminous brown skin unmarked by any kind of gooseflesh.

The fog obscures the doorway, and filaments weave around the four.

'I will initially translate for us,' says the tūrehu, and everything Gran said about their music is true. I hear song in these ordinary words. 'We are the five signatories to our objection to the proposed –'

The sharky lawyer is on his feet. 'Mister Mayor Mister Mayor if I may –'

The Mayor's hands are rigidly flat on the table.

'What is it Mr Reiver?' His voice is hoarse.

'If these these – things arnt hoaxes, they arnt human either!'

The tūrehu turns its head towards him and smiles, placidly.

But the lawyer takes a quick step backwards and bangs into his chair.

I can see the smile too. Someone who smiles like that would slice your belly open to check what you had for breakfast, quite playfully and just in the interests of learning. Then they'd tie your intestines in a bow –

'Your objection is rather similar to that which you raised apropos the material our submission was written on. The council has not been specific about what an objection should be written upon, nor has it been specific as to whether objectors speaking to their submissions have to be human. Or not.'

The smile widens a little.

'Happily, we are not.'

'But, but, there's only four of you and –'

'You really wouldn't like the other one of us to come in here with you. Besides he wouldn't ah, fit. See?'

And every eye – except for those of the Others – follows the long slim finger as it swings to the doorway.

There is a wonderful arc, scimitar curve, rearing out of the mist. It is dark, massive, tall as the door, and ends in a point so sharp it can't be clearly seen. It flexes once.

I really really wouldn't like whatever owns that claw to be in here with me.

Nor would anyone else, judging by the absolute silence.

The lawyer slithers bonelessly down on his chair, and the tūrehu turns its head back to the council table.

'We are the five signatories to our objection to the planned roading development and subdivision of the land you know as the Neck. The maeroero and his daughter will speak first.'

'Signatories?' squeaked the lawyer. His sharkliness was gutted, gone, but he was still trying his nastiest. Which I admired, deepdown. I wasn't game to do anything except stare, and breathe occasionally. O, and make a note or two.

'The maeroero and his daughter have signed their names in their language, there being no requirement from the council for English or Māori only to be used for such matters. He is Third-stop and she is Sixth, and you will note the finger directions quite plainly in the two lines of holes at the lefthand bottom end of the flax leaf.'

I see Sam actually check.

'I thought they were nibblings by insects.' No-one can hear her, but I know the ways of her lips.

The lawyer slumps a little more. Soamy isn't smirking any more. You can't when your mouth is hanging open.

The tūrehu's smile is beatific.

The two red giants stand a little straighter. One of them farts. We hear the shells tinkle. Then the male lifts the femur-flute and breathes into it. The female opens her mouth and croons.

Is there something narcotic in that damned fog?

It's like quiet tuneful moaning: only it seeps into you and makes you feel vague and sad.

Then you feel – words, words stroking your skin, fingering the inner drums of your ears.

We were here first. We have never left. We own our homelands.

We prefer to be in the shadows. We roam the lands at night.

We were on the Almost-island before you came, it has always been ours.

We will remain there, in company with the first arrivals.

We share with them but not with humans. Go away. Leave us alone.

It seems the flute and crooning have come to an end, although I can still hear the music in my head.

Many of the gobsmacked councillors twitch, shoot terrified – or bovinely puzzled – looks at each other.

'I see I do not have to translate in this instance,' says the tūrehu smoothly. Its English is as inhumanly perfect as everything else about it. 'A ponaturi from the Poutini horde will now speak on behalf of her kind. The signature is that nail scrape to the right of the maeroero signatures.' The tūrehu twinkles in a kindly fashion to Reischek's sunken lawyer who has turned quite yellow. 'It is an old ponaturi clan name meaning "May your throat be quickly slashed", thought appropriate in this instance.'

Ponaturi, ponaturi? Gran had never said much about them, unlike her stories about the bush fairies whom she dearly loved, but I dimly recall it was all terrifying. A clever and vindictive seafolk, who killed humans much more often than humans killed them (although our stories didn't exactly emphasise this).

Note: ponaturi nails are long, strong-looking, and savagely pointed.

The ponaturi's speech goes on for many painful minutes, slashing at all our ears. It crackles and hisses, sounds like highpitched static mixed with strata of loathing and spat hate.

'That was a very brief recital of interactions between ponaturi and humans over the past eight centuries. Most of them concern the previous owners of the land, of whom Mr Auhei was such an eloquent and definitive representative.'

Ouch.

'However, three incidents specifically relate to direct line ancestors of the Mayor, a councillor, and the applicant land-developer.'

How can you make *applicant land-developer* sound like a tiny perfect lullaby?

The ponaturi grates and sizzles again.

'Mister Mayor, your paternal ancestor of three generations ago fired at a ponaturi of Clan Gut in the dark and loudly claimed he had shot a demmed native. Any similarity between a New Zealander and a ponaturi is, I think you would agree, negligible?'

The Mayor nods, numbly.

More hate speech.

'As well as the insult your ancestor delivered, his bullet severely grazed the ponaturi's back. This means there is a blood issue between Clan Gut and any and all lineal descendants of your ancestors. 'Your life is forfeit and you are unable to make any objective decision on any matter arising from disputes between ponaturi and humans, according to ponaturi law. As the Neck is an ancient place of refuge for ponaturi ... I do not have to spell it out, do I?'

'That isn't our rules,' says the Mayor, in a very small voice.

'O sometimes, the older laws have their place. The Poutini ponaturi have delivered due warning to you. They do take everything so personally you know. A rather young and hasty folk.' The tūrehu can do confidential smiles too.

'We are also informed that the grandfather of Councillor Mooch'

'Eh? Wot?'

'distaff side, cast urine on the person of a peaceable net-mender working on shore in the late evening. The fact that your ancestor was blind drunk does not exculpate him. Or you. Such insults are a deadly serious matter with the ponaturi clans, and you are in the same unfortunate position as your Mayor.'

'Eh! Wot!'

'Annnd, Mister Reischek? According to the ponaturi – I will testify that they have accurate memories beyond the guess or conception of humans – one of your female ancestors, four generations back on your mother's side, fell upon an innocent young ponaturi, wandering in a carefree fashion down Sevenmile Beach, minding his own business, and slaked her drunken lust upon him. My goodness, you were a jolly lot back then weren't you? My interpolation – the ponaturi do not have this view of you. Regrettably however, your greatgreatgrandmother was a goldfields prostitute and some kind of cross-species infect –'

'That is a bloody lie!' Soamy is a florid flabby man but he has sprung to his feet quite pale and taut.

Hmm. Note: check out some of the older generations' gossip. Possible goldmine here.

'Bloody bloody lies! Bloody bloody *things*! This a bloody travesty this this this –' spitting sputtering incoherency as he rushes towards the ponaturi knocking chairs aside.

The ponaturi very distinctly sneers. She spreads her long-nailed hands –

and that huge claw in the doorway – scraped.

My teeth shuddered. Several people clapped hands over their ears and others were shivering. Reischek has fallen to the floor, whether tripped or crashed is uncertain.

'There is corroboration, or should I say, belief in the facts as stated? This is not regarded a matter of morality by the ponaturi, but as an absolute case for war. Very particular about their gene pool, these folk.' The tūrehu beamed. 'So. The gist of the ponaturi submission is that, should a decision detrimental to their continued occupation of the sanctuary of the Neck be made by this council, war will be declared upon you all and everybody you have any dealing with.'

Everyone round the council table, and longside in the petitioners' chairs, is looking strangely blank.

More crackling and clatter from the ponaturi.

'O, and in the interests of a fair fight' musical laughter bubbles under those words 'they wish you to know they are no longer susceptible to sunlight and they have cultivated many new ah, pets. Yes, pets. I particularly like the little leggy ones with pretty blue rings now so well adapted to cold waters, but most of them are *much* smaller.'

It is right then I notice that the tūrehu has no pupils to its eyes either. Just ultimate fathomless green ... I notice this because it is smiling now at me.

You ever felt your anal sphincter *crunch* shut? And then twist?

'You are still hearing us, aren't you?'

'Uh. Uh. Yes.'

The tūrehu sighs, a sigh with a rirerire trill running under it.

'Well, we tried. We are going now. You probably won't ever see us again.'

'Oh no! I mean, what about –'

'Hmmm?'

'Your submission? And your signature? And and –'

'I am a simple co-ordinator. My signature? The flax leaf of

course. The taniwha has officially breathed on the whole. We sympathise entirely with both given submissions.'

'But going before the summary and the vote and –'

'We came because we thought seeing us clearly might cause wonder, make you realise there is much more than you think you know about our world. We thought our very presence might open minds and change present attitudes. All of us heard most minds snap shut minutes ago.'

'Not mine,' whispers Sam, very pale Sam.

'Nor your friend's,' answers the tūrehu. 'Do give my regards to your grandmother by the way. We spent a happy afternoon together some time ago. She was a charming child.'

'She died twenty years ago.'

'O well. That is the way with you folk isn't it? Something of her thinking must have been given to you because you can still see and think. Look at the others.'

The Mayor is staring at the fog.

Councillor Alley has slumped under the table. No other councillor is moving, all sitting hunched and stone-faced except Councillor Mooch and he's back on automatic again. The general manager is staring at his sheaf of papers and his secretary's eyes are tight shut. There is no sign of Reischek or his lawyer.

'Is – this – real?' I ask the tūrehu.

'As real as your life,' it answers, 'and as real as whatever you call reality. It is just that your kind can't stand very much reality. You much prefer your patterns and your stories and your noisy dirty tramplings over everything. However, you don't last forever and we almost do. We are going now. I would go quite soon too, if I were you,' and it gives a small smile and, horrifyingly, winks. And the mist and Others weren't there any more.

Being bored seemed such a desirable state. While Sam and I twitched and quivered, the Mayor and councillors jerked – well 'awake' is as good as any other word here I suppose, and went into recess on the grounds of commercial sensitivity.

I wrote a bland report of the meeting, précising the submissions against the development of the Neck. 'Emphasis was placed by all objectors on the desirability of keeping the Neck in its present state, with some supporting takata whenua concerns and others wanting protection for endangered invertebrates. However, it is unlikely the Council will give great weight to these matters when' te mea te mea blah blah blah.

A week later, the paper prints a picture of the Mayor and Soamy smiling into the camera, shaking hands across a display, an artist's conception of the tasteful eco-friendly village Reischek planned to build.

Then Sam and I sold what we had and fled to the other side of the hill.

We drove past the Neck on our way out. It is a large peninsula, with a high, forested headland. There are seaviews all the way round, seaviews to die for. We know about the deep lake nested in the middle of the thousand hectare plateau, and had learned that birdlife abounds. All of it unclaimed Crown land and nobody else near it, loving it, except for a few old hippies on a rundown ohu to the north, and a wet-eyed environmentalist and a grumpy lover of silence to the south. You could see immediately why a developer would take one look and see CASH OPPORTUNITY in high golden letters. And that would be all he saw.

The news isn't good from what remains of the Coast. Last summer's toxic algae blooms killed off all the salmon farms and ruined the last whitebait season. The goo that developed suddenly in their sewage ponds and sewerage was a huge problem, swelling the contents a thousandfold overnight. I heard Soamy was one of the first fatalities, overwhelmed by a surge from the Hurihuri system as he was out walking his dog one night. Confirmation was pretty hard to come by – and I really wanted to know what happened to the dog – because, by then, the permanent rain had wrecked almost every bridge and length of hill road there was. It had done things you wouldn't believe to electric and 'tronic systems everywhere over there. And finally, the earthquake swarms began –

They are creatures of mist and rain and aloneness
says my gran
they play water and sadness into our world
she said.
They are people of cunning and malice, and sunshine and music and stillness

says my gran

they bring together all of the Others, the ancient unborn, the young and the old

she said.

And never forget the dwellers-in-water, shape-shifters, changers

says my gran

and that all of them hate us strangers, who came from the Abyssal Void

yes, I do remember what she said.

And I thought it was just one of Gran's little songs. Now I teach it to our children.

Sam and I live quietly by a far southern lake. I'm a good gardener and she is a good harvester of weka and fish. Life is strenuous and much less certain than it used to be, but we are never bored.

And we hope each evening, while listening to the winds play like flutes in the far mountains and watching the flax bushes sway,

we hope the Coast was enough.

Storehouse for the Hungry Ghosts

CALL THEM NGĀTI NOBODY because for a long time they never admitted what they had done. Or, if they said Yes, it was our old men who takahi'd the islands and knocked a few heads in, so what? They never admitted they had done anything wrong. Or, if they said, Well, it wasn't a nice thing to do, but that's the way it was then, everybody behaved like that, there was nothing wrong with it, right? They never admitted they were responsible for all that happened after.

Even the piano-case man, even his thirty-five stone.

It wasn't an easy life. The weather gnawed you. On those rare days when the wind didn't blow, the entire population would come out and lie on the sunward slopes, and go to sleep. Men and women and children, like seals, warming their bones. They knew well enough they couldn't let their numbers grow beyond the chancy food resources, but they are the only people I have heard of who controlled their numbers by castrating a certain number of boy infants – a pleasant change from the infanticide of girls. They didn't like killing people. If arguments couldn't be resolved by words or magic, they whacked away at one another with quarter-staffs and stopped as soon as someone showed blood. They loved life, and they were good at it. It was more than a pity so many had to die.

They called him 'the Last'. That's how I knew of him. So-and-so.

Te mea te mea. The Last of The … no, not Mohicans. It's depressing, isn't it, how many peoples some lonely soul has been 'The Last of'. Anyway, that's how history books called him. And they mentioned the packing case that had held a piano. Had to use that, not a conventional coffin, because he was a big BIG man.

Some of the books I read when I was young even mentioned his specially-trained draught mare that, while he could still ride, used to plod stolidly round the island, past the illustrated trees, past the sand dunes where the seated dead, the honourably-buried ones, appeared when the wind blew their blankets off, past the ovens and the gnawed and strewn bones.

But the books never told me what he truly was. It takes dreams to tell you that.

There are two dozen scones fat with butter. The golden syrup runs stickily over their edges. He is calm and precise about picking them up, biting them in half, chewing them twice, and swallowing, one swallow to half a scone, forty-eight swallows for the smoko snack. His hands are plump, he is neat-fingered. His brown eyes twinkle. He has a warm rich smile. He calls for another pot of tea, and another bowl of sugar.

The old writers, the really old writers, the ones from the eighteenth century, mention the people's merriment, their good humour. 'The People of the Sun' was an early christening, but they just called themselves tchakat henu, people of the land. We still do that, all of us here – tangata whenua, Earth people. And yet, we're islanders, habitants of the sea as much as the good earth. Maybe it's because we hope our bones will rest easy in the ground, rather than in the belly of a shark?

It is a fine fat fore-quarter of lamb, a prime beast off his own farm. He slices one juicy pink slice after another until the ivory bone is exposed all the way round. He eats each slice.

His guest sits still, stupefied with food. They had shared the first haunch, and he had particularly enjoyed the perfection of the roast, crisp skin of fat, and melting meat. They ate largely also of the kūmara and the fresh sweet peas, and he could only accept a token half dozen slices of the second haunch. He's a big man, the guest, but he had stared at the renewed pile of vegetables and sighed.

The man known as The Last Of puts down the bone. He smiles.

'Whakarawa has made us plum-duff. Do you like the cream poured on yours, or separate in the jug?'

They had unusual boats, the tchakat henu. The waves washed through them. They looked makeshift and rough. Like the people they were largely undecorated – no elaborate carvings or ornaments, no inspiring of awe, no arrogant splendour. They were practical, *useful*, crafts, made to travel fifty or more kilometres between rough-rocked islands, made to endure whatever a cold restless sea could do to them, made to anchor in the kelp-beds while their owners fished or landed on the nursery islands.

On the nursery islands: taiko chicks, albatross chicks, bird chicks rotund with creamy smooth fat, ruru and para and tataki. Countless thousands of fat chicks so carefully harvested that there're plenty left today.

There's pain and cruelty in everything:

> *each bird as he extracts it, he breaks the thighbones of,*
> *interlocks the wings, forces the upper mandible through*
> *the V of the lower to seal the beak and prevent oilsoil*
> *of the feathers for ease of plucking, and goes home. There*
> *he hangs up his birds in bunches waiting*
> *to be plucked, the while the ambience vibrates with*
> *the wails of bird agony …*

There's pain and cruelty in everything. Did not my own tribe keep slaves, even slaves of The People of The Sun? Do I not tell you this story, giving you images you don't necessarily want, griefs that are old, old, and irremediable?

But the fat, the fat of those chicks! Up to an inch thick, of the most delicate and silken and digestible nature!

He sits in the afternoon sun, the case of tomatoes gleaming by his hand. He talks, continuously: his conversation is funny without being raucous, his gossip witty rather than caustic. He has been making sausages for several hours, and while most of them have been given away, the family is cooking up many dozen for tea. The good feeling of having grown and harvested your own food; the better feeling to have shared it; the best feeling, to eat to repletion with your family. He nibbles another plump red globe and notices with mild surprise, that's the last one? Ah well, send Bully for another case, there's plenty more.

They remembered for many years the names of the many dead from Tamakaroro killed by sailors from the brig *Chatham*, to the quartermile long line of corpses laid on the beach at Waitangi by Tikaokao and his men … a neat mode of killing, most agreed, a whack with the blunt end of a tomahawk to the temple, fine when you have a passive foe, a foe that doesn't fight back ...

They remembered for many years the many dead until the living grew too few. Now we have lists, and piles of skulls with holes in the temples, and no way of knowing who was who.

He sat one night in a grove of kōpī trees and watched the little figures graven in the bark begin to dance their names. It was dark, late night, but the dancing figures are bright as the moon. He thought of the ways whereby a man would prove his strength and courage in the days gone forever.

He could show the courage of patience by making a hafted adze.

He could show the courage of daring landing a boat by a wave-battered *concave* rockface, or clambering over the perilous birding-cliffs. He could show the courage of endurance and skill by diving into the cold seas and not surfacing until he had a crayfish in either hand, and another clenched between his jaws. He knows already how to show chiefly generosity: he is naturally gifted with stamina and great strength: it is the mid-1920s and he is a successful and wealthy farmer, loved as well as respected by all who know him.

But black-fish are forever stranding on the shore in his dreams, and even birdsong is sometimes drowned by the chattering of teeth.

The little bright figures are very still on the kōpī trees.

If I could ever time-travel, back down the line of ancestors, I would make certain to take with me a dentist with a well-equipped surgery. I have seen too many old skulls with pits and corrosions from jaw abscesses and rotted teeth. And the skulls were only old in the sense that they came from centuries past; the owners had been in their twenties and thirties. Soft foods weren't common, and were greatly relished, for teeth got chipped or worn down, and infections crept into the bones so quick. Strange, isn't it? We die from overeating, many of us, but it's bloody rare to find anyone dying these days because they have bad teeth. We take flour and rice and butter and cheese and prime meat with no splinters in it as natural everyday fare. Potatoes and pasta and a hundred ways with a hundred different kinds of fish, fresh or cleanly frozen or soft and hygienic in tins … and cooking pots and pans, and ovens, not to mention microwaves.

I spent a week, once, living on what I could catch or collect, and cooking the lot in seaweed bags, or in taopīpī. I had planned to do it for a month, but I already had two chipped teeth and a vast new appreciation of modern day life.

And I'd cheated.

I took along a hipflask of whisky, and two chocolate bars.

The law of Nunuku, as we know it, goes like this.

For now and forever
Never again let there be war
From today, forget the taste of human flesh
May your bowels rot the day
You disobey this injunction.

They were a holy people, a very tapu people, a people bound by law, and over the centuries they abided by the injunction of Nunukuwhenua. And their bowels remained unrotted, at least during their short short lives.

Those who weren't arbitrarily hit on the head, killed for the oven, or rendered lifeless by violations of their tapu, were enslaved. And some days food was a sandy raw potato, and some days food was a bone the dogs ignored. And all around were the unburied dead, only occasionally secretly lamented. For years, to live was to despair.

I do not forget that the whites stood aside and did nothing. I do not forget that measles and influenza and syphilis killed more than the cunning effortlessly-wielded tomahawks of Ngāti Nobody.

I do not blame anybody, because I wasn't alive then, and, given my background, would either have been smacking holes in temples or quietly looking on.

I just wonder about the man who was 'The Last'. The man who ate himself to death.

He always put his appetite down to the fact that he was reared on condensed milk. He smiled his vivid and lovely smile as he retold this fact.

See the English surgeon strolling along the beach. He has a little hammer; his servant, a reverential pace behind him, has a little bag. The land is bathed in sunshine, but there's nobody else lolling around enjoying it.

Fine incisors, beautiful molars, thinks the English surgeon, and will ye look at that? More perfect front teeth I have never seen. Tap, tap. He drops the broken eggshell skull. Dentures, he considers, properly fitted, five guineas a set, minimum, for the quality. Clitter, clitter. He smiles happily, and his assistant smiles a sycophantic smile (with any fuckin' luck we'll get off the fuckin' *Harriet* and straight into a cushy berth) clutching the little bag nearly atop with fifty guineas worth.

O yes. By 1835, flour and potatoes had superseded ground

bracken root, and teeth had never been better.

The only time people recorded seeing the big man angry was nearly a century later. He was dieting. Did the importunings of his family, who loved him dearly, finally beat down his resolve? He was dieting: no fat on the meat, no butter on the bread. He was dieting: he knew in his heart it was useless but the family … and the clash of desires of priorities of needs rose a red cloud in his head puffing his face out monstrously and making the veins knot in his neck and fists. He whips the table cloth out from under all the plates, the cutlery, the crockery, everyone else's gravyrich heaped-up dishes and the whole lot crashes into the sudden silence.

The kōpī groves have dwindled away, and there are few drawings left. The family of The Last grows and grows. In numbers and mana and standing it grows.

He Waiata Tangi Mō Tama Rehe. 'The Last of the Moriori.'

> He told himself one dark night,
> *'all that has been, lives,*
> *good and bad' and so he ate:*
> *fat chicks of albatross, haunches of young lambs*
> *plum puddings whole and bread that swam in butter*
> *a sea of crayfish and an underground hall*
> *of kūmara: sugar sweet, whisky neat, all the largess*
> *of the world; he swelled, and swelled until*

heavy with memories of placid surfeit
he tipped the scales into the grave.
'I am rich with good things and the poor ghosts
shall not be sent
empty away'

Afternote

If you are interested in reading more of the true, though hotly denied by many Māori, tragic story of the Moriori of the Chatham Islands, the book to go to is *Moriori – A People Rediscovered*, by Michael King, published Viking Penguin, 1989.

I used to be fairly smug about the whole affair. I knew they hadn't died out because one of my school mates was of Moriori descent and It Was North Islanders That Did It!

Then I learned that my people, Kai Tahu, had accepted a pair of Moriori slaves in the 1840s, and that on a cousin line in my own whakapapa is a Moriori who escaped from the hellhole of the Auckland Islands and settled in Murihiku. 'Nothing human is alien to me', but when anything comes that close to home, the ghosts begin to stir and work like yeast in your dreams.

Hatchings

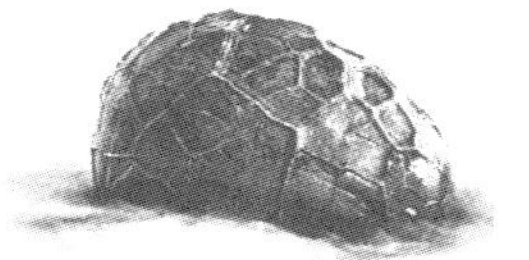

FIFTY YEARS, she is thinking, fifty years ago.

– You're sure you'll be okay Mum?

She nods.

– I'm not the one who had the heart attack. I'll be fine.

She says it briskly, knowing he is reassured by a lack of sentimentality.

She doesn't feel brisk. It's all that weight of days. He was twelve: I was thirty-two.

Carlin comes over and airkisses her cheek. Her perfume is subtle, her make-up immaculate.

– Ring us every day. We'll come again next weekend.

– Thank you dear.

– You've got your alarm on?

She holds it up, silently.

– Such a comfort. It must give you real peace of mind.

She smiles, nods. No, it doesn't. Gives you two peace of mind though. I suppose it's worth it for that. A button that rings a number and has someone ask me if I'm alright, and rings an ambulance if there's no reply or the wrong reply … takes forty-five minutes to get here. Be a bit late, I'm thinking –

– Mum? Yes or no?

– What?

– I said, do you want us to bring Uncle Dave out next time? Are you really feeling alright?

– *I* am feeling fine. You take good care of your*self.* You take good care of him too, Carlin. And no, don't bring Dave, he's too confused. He still thinks Jim is around planting trees somewhere instead of feeding 'em.

– Oooh Mum!

But they seem convinced that there is nothing wrong with her.

And there isn't really, as she waves goodbye until their car is lost in the dust near the bend of the road. Just a bit tired. Nothing a little lie-down won't fix.

But first –

the home stand is only three hundred yards from the house. Jim had planted it before they had shifted from the city, coming here on his weekends, digging holes for the spindly gums, planting them at ten foot intervals. So, when she and the twelve year olds finally arrived in the late autumn

– my goodness, was it really fifty years ago? A whole half century? And this is all that's left of all that work?

two hundred slender trees made a patch of aromatic shade. Not deep shade, not like real bush, but a good place to be in during the still Peninsula summer heat. She often walked out here, especially in the later afternoon, especially after she learned their ways. Used to take a couple of minutes.

I am getting so slow at everything.

The ringing noise is in her ears, so she leans against the nearest trunk until it stops.

And then she listens intently.

Sight might be going, just a bit, but hearing's as good as ever.

She can't hear anything except the rustle of leaves, the quiet scratch of dangling scraps of bark.

She plods back to the house, stopping – as always – to look down into the little bay where her greatgrandfather had been casked, and nod, silently. We still forget his name, Pōua –

The ticking is loud here. Must be four or five of them on the go.

Make a cuppa? Yes, make a cuppa.

Am I talking out loud?

Don't know. Don't care.

She moves heavily around the stark kitchen, glad she had got rid of most of the furniture, furnishings, after Jim had died. It makes things easier somehow. Less stuff to look after. Just enough for comfort. She takes the cup of tea through to her bedroom, and sits down in the La-z-boy by the deepsilled double window.

The sound is like energetic mice gnawing wood. It isn't steady: sometimes it's just one mouse, then two or three, then a little space of silence as they pause and gather more strength.

Over the years, she has learned their rhythms. Almost always they begin in the afternoon. Of course, there's the odd one which starts in the morning, and she's had more than a few that begin in the deep of night.

But most of 'em, most of 'em –

The scratchy gnawing goes on –

She looks at the tea. There's dusty scum on top and it is cold.

Nodded off again eh? O well.

She drinks it anyway. To go out to the kitchen and boil the jug and rinse the mug and make another cuppa –

And notices, on one of the branches with dry leaves, a dry leaf that isn't.

She is annoyed at herself. Every birth is new life in the world and she wouldn't willingly miss one.

It is a male, his russet plumes absolutely still, and he is still until an instinct from the deep past sets him briefly moving, like a dead leaf trembling in the breeze.

She knows, now, something of evolutionary theory and still can't understand much of it. Raw stuff, she thinks, another story we tell ourselves. Cause it does make a sort of sense. The ones that had come to look like dead leaves, and had acted like dead leaves, lived to breed offspring. Who did the same thing. Or, if they didn't, didn't leave offspring. Because there they were in daylight, and if they showed life, something with sharp teeth or a pointy beak saw food. And that was that.

It's the strange subtleties that bother her. There are females who imitate dead leaves too, but differently. *They* let their forewings cover the startling eyespots and angle their abdomens to the left. The abdomen has a single dark stripe towards the end which matches the dark pattern round the edge of the left forewing. And suddenly, there's no longer a plumpbellied treat hanging from a twig: there is an old leaf, notched with rot, obviously inedible –

but the moth can never have seen the effect, she thinks, puzzled all over again, it's never been a moth before. They say it's just a lucky chance effect, genetically encoded, that helps the species survive. Anything at all can come about over the thousands and thousands of years.

She's seen changes in them over her lifetime here. Moths that had always been shades of brown – sepia, dun, tawny – have begun to develop greenish sheens. Our eucalypts stay mainly green in the hottest summer ...

One of the branches in the far pottery urn is shivering: the inch-long brown cylinder opens at the up-stem end. Ah hah, thin antennae and fat fat body, as the female crawls quickly, somehow jerkily desperate, out of the cocoon and up to the end of the branch to rest. Brown fluid squirts from the end of her abdomen, and then she positions her tarsii and stills. The growths at her sides look tumorous.

And then the magic begins ...

She never tires of the watching. Right from the first year when she learned what lived in Jim's trees.

He hated them. Well, they did eat the gum leaves. But that wasn't any cause to burn her moth diaries. Dunno why, she thinks. Tho' he came back strange and he got stranger. Wasn't all his fault though. He never did let on what happened over there, never did tell her anything. Maybe talked to his mates down at the RSA each year, drunken after the Dawn Parade was long over, but not ever to her. Could sort of understand it. I just brought up the babies. He was killing people and getting hurt. I think that's what it was. Maybe. But I could never find a way to really talk – I mean, I never even talked to him about my family. And he never asked anything –

he had taken to sleeping on the front verandah after they'd been here for two years.

– You don't want me? I'm your wife. I'm your helpmate.

Silence.

– You don't want more babies? I can –

– Twins!

He grated it out.

– Like fukkin rats. Pups. Litters. Things.

So, no more babies.

She still regrets that. The twins were so different, one – what did they say? A control freak, that was it, with an innate skill at managing, manipulating people. She'd rode a family story all the way to a top job at the United Nations. And the other a gentle passive man, uninterested in stories family or otherwise, content to settle down with the love of his life, and work steadily, unadventurously, as a public service accountant until retirement came.

At least he still has the love of his life, she thinks sadly. It was different for us –

he'd come in at seven for his porridge and tea and bacon and eggs, never changed. I'd always have it ready. Then he'd pick up his thermos and sandwich tin and away he'd go, fencing or planting or helping out on neighbouring farms. The twins were at boarding school then and rarely home. But always plenty to do. I was gardening for us and down-the-road, and looking after the chooks and the goats and planting my bush.

That took up my time. Thought that'd be a small paradise for us in our old age. For the grandkids, and maybe *their* kids …

Home and garden and trees and animals – what more could a body want?

Knowing, she thinks, really knowing.

Really knowing what happens.

And not being sad that the family finishes with us. Had he seen that end? Pōua who came out so changed, they said, no-one could believe it was the same warrior and politician who had been – incaskerated was the word my slightly cruel daughter used. A dreadful thing for one human to do to another. We are not lovely beings, she decides, watching the imperceptibly slow unfurling of the wings.

She'd written,

'I found your name in your book at the library. I am writing to the address at the front. I hope you get this letter. I am very interested in the insects we have on our farm and you wrote so lovingly about them. I would like to know more. I attained Proficiency but nothing further. Please tell me where I can look. I can send postage.' She enclosed the only moth diary that remained. She hadn't really expected an answer, just hoped. The elderly man with tufty white hair on the dust-jacket had looked kind.

The house was nearly silent of live human voices. She kept the radio on all day but Jim hated it at night. He'd eat tea, chops or a stew, rarely steak and never sausages ('You don't want to know *what's* in *them*'), potatoes, and peas or carrots and silver beet. While eating pudding, he might comment on how everything was too dry and we mustn't expect any rain, or that he had reposted and wired three chain over at Kelvey's, or planted another fifty trees in the long paddock plantation. It was his way of saying thank you for the food, for her being there, she thought. But she would have loved more talk.

She always made time, whatever the weather, to go out to the main gate and wait for the mailvan. The driver was a cheerful young man, and happily spent a couple of minutes in chat. – You shouldn't be out in this rain missus! Not much today either, couple of accounts, the *Farmers' News*, letter from her in New York, that's about it.

Except one bright afternoon in 1972 he grins widely and waves a thick rectangular package at her. – Feels like really heavy reading here!

'Dear Mrs Lex' – the letter was typed except for the greeting and signature – 'I was grateful for the opportunity to read your carefully kept observations on the *Antheraea eucalypti* pupa hatchings (enclosed). I note the cover dates, January 1954–February 1958, and wonder whether you may have other records? Would you be prepared to share them? It is important that precise observations come from as broad a range of interested nature-lovers as possible, whether lay people like yourself or professional scientists. This is the way we learn and get to really know how Nature works.'

She can still recall the happiness, and the way her hands shook as she read. Even the smell of the fresh polish on the wooden table where The Book lay.

He wrote, the kindly tufty whitehaired man, that the best work he could send her in the meantime was a recent compilation by a colleague.

'... particularly for the generous section he has on the moth so dear to you. You may have come across his words regarding the importance of lay observation? "A scientist, however dedicated, can not observe everything. We are fortunate to have many keen nature lovers in this country who can provide us with invaluable information."

'With my best regards and a hope that you will consider sending more observations to those of us who will appreciate them.'

She had written back within the week, explaining that the other moth diaries had met with an accident but she would faithfully keep and send more.

The letter came back stamped Deceased.

There was a late summer when Jim had finally lost all restraint. He had taken the slasher to her mānuka grove, ringbarked the young tōtara, and tried to kill the fleet goats. Set fire to the back porch and swung the slasher at her. She had fled to down-the-road. Ringing her son in Wellington before the police, then ringing her daughter in New York before the doctor. Glad she had. And, later, felt only dull relief when the doctor committed Jim to Sunnyside. She had journeyed over the hills to the city for many weekends, only to be faced each time by a stranger purple-faced with rage even though sedated and under restraint. Eventually, his only family, his brother Dave said, It just makes him worse. Maybe it would be better –

It took a decade for his head to explode from that rage.

Pōua must have felt rage, more than I can ever imagine. He was used to battle, had killed other men in hand-to-hand combat. Her mother had showed them the whalebone-handled tomahawk which her pōua sunk into the skulls of at least two Gati Laki when they raided south. She still feels a pang when she thinks about where the deadly little axe is now – in a scraped grave somewhere in the North African desert, guarding her brother's bones. But Pōua can't have had it to hand when the whaler crew jumped him. And to think of him coming to, his hands bound behind him, body doubled and crammed into a whale-oil cask with its top nailed on, and only a fist-sized hole in the side for air. Why, the entire cask must have shuddered with his trapped rage!

– Ooof. Her head has slumped hard on her chest.

Dunno why I keep falling asleep like this. Look, another three hatched and their wings already expanded. All perfect thank goodness.

◆

There had been a dreadful season two years ago, just after she sold the last but one planted block. The new owners had razed gumtrees for firewood, and then sprayed the stumped ground with some unnamed poison. Spray must have drifted across to the home plantation because many of the cocoons she gathered were misshapen and didn't hatch out, and most of the ones that did – she wishes they hadn't. Some had stumps for legs or no antennae, and several, wings that remained crumpled and truly tumorous. She had taken all the monsters outside after the others had flown and put them gently on the gumleaf-heaped ground. She hoped the owls or possums took them quite soon.

There's a strangeness just hatched, but I've seen its like before. Its ambiguity has nothing to do with poisons: it is a natural occurrence. Instead of a male's plumes, it has antennae almost as narrow as a female, but its body isn't a fat pouch of eggs. It is a dapper little male-lookalike, with a male's line of black spots on either side of its abdomen, and a male's camouflage techniques.

– But I've seen this kind before and I know they lack entirely a male's interest in females. There are Carlins in all species and maybe they have her gentle and generous nature.

– I'd love to give you grandkids …

– It's alright my dear. What is meant to be is meant to be.

It was what my mum used to say. And, forgive, but never forget.

◆

Dunno why I think of that now –

of course Mum didn't mean us to do that about the whalerman's name. Scrub him out of memory, out of history, but remember his deed.

Remember his arrogance and treachery, and remember how your greatgrandfather was changed.

Three weeks in a whaleoil tun, cramped, stinking, hungry, thirst quenched with a tin mug of water twice a day. It took him, the family story went, a day and a night to free his hands, and the jeering whalers simply tipped the water over him until he could take the cup. When they took off the top of the cask, yelling insults and, You won't do that again blackie! they stilled into silence. Pōua's hair had turned white but his eyes were huge and glowed. He stood slowly, without assistance, looked at the silent crew and said, You will all be dead before this moon is dead. He walked into the tide and swam until he was clean, and then waited quietly at the end of the little peninsula until his people came.

– But why didn't they come before? she remembers asking at the same moment her brother asked, Did all the whalers die? Their mother sighed. We were told that the wicked men were smashed by a whale they had struck, but not the one who ordered the deed. He fled to the north. And why didn't we come to Pōua's aid at once? I don't know. All I do know is that afterwards, Pōua could call all his people without opening his mouth. He could tell when any of us were going to die. He knew to the day how long he would live. And he said he wouldn't be forgotten but his foe would never be remembered except for his deed.

Well, that is sort of true. My daughter was horrified by the injustice.

– But all he did was not tell the whalers a taua was on the way! He didn't have any obligation to tell *them*! And she, with a crackly new degree and knowing much more than her mum and my mum, went through old documents and found out the head whaler's name. I refused to hear it, and her brother smiled but immediately forgot. In the angry active years that followed, she used our story and used our story and wound up heading some big commission here, and a bigger one over in America. She hasn't come back home …

Some of the twenty or so moths are flexing their wings. It is getting dark.

Must open the window soon.

She looks at the gum stalks upright in the small heavy pots. With a practised eye, she checks off which have hatched – all except that one over there, and as she eyes it, hears it start to tick.

Shaking her head. Old niddlenoddle you, still captivated by the changes that lead to this moment. Mustard-seed egg to thin thread of black caterpillar, and many moults later, the final instar, a regal beast, long as her forefinger, green along the sides, with yellow stripes and many small orange and red tubercles, but turquoisey on top and crowned with bright blue jewels …and this wonder loses its voracious appetite at last, and darkens; in an almost apathetic way, seeks a suitable twig and begins to spin a weatherproof retreat, pouring out its caterpillarhood into a shelter for its next new self. And after many months of lying, a varnished brown pupa (she has seen photos but never had the heart to cut open a cocoon) the last change begins. The moth-to-be begins to turn in its casket. That is the ticking, that is the start –

this one is working urgently, with no rest breaks, almost as though it knows it is last to hatch. She can see a neat line, beginning of a circle. So it will be a male: the females make a larger ragged exit.

I should go and have something to eat.

Can always do that afterwards.

All those changes, with chances to die at every one: insects and birds can eat the yellow eggs, stripping off the single row on a leaf with relish. She has seen spiders take the small caterpillars, and a starling peck a larger one. The cocoons can fail to hatch, and owls take the adult moths before they have a chance to breed.

Auē, so much effort only to fail at the last.

Staring at the last hatching cocoon and suddenly Jim's face is above the twigs. He's chewing something: she sees his fork loaded with egg and bacon. He raises his eyebrows at her, and fades. But there are still large eyes looking at her, and a bright corona –

She shivers. Don't want to go funny in the head. She shuts her eyes hard, and when she opens them, there are just the moths and the pots and the ticking twig. That's alright then, she thinks, heart still thudding – and it was better to see breakfast-Jim than the madman, frothing and screaming. Or the pallid empty-faced body.

She hoped then, hopes now, that some part of him found peace. That all the manic driven work of planting eucalypts and working on other people's farms had a reward beyond that of jobs accomplished, wages earned. Most of the wages went on buying more trees, almost a forestful, and now there is only the home plantation left. She knows her son will keep it as a sanctuary for as long as he lives.

Two of the moths are rattling at the windows.

She raises herself heavily, and opens the catch, pushes the left window ajar. As she sits down hard, the big moths begin to flit away.

– Bye bye darlings. Find each other, breed well.

She sighs. The last one still hasn't hatched, is still ticking. Well, I can wait. Think I'll just have a little sleep meantime –

Kissing It As It Flies

SO, HERE WE ARE,

a happy never after family,

being more or less together in the sunshine.

– Tell me again, because I was a baby then wasn't I?

– Yes. You were four months old.

– And Josh was ten?

– That's right, the same age as Ari.

– But that wasn't his name really.

– Well, it was and it wasn't. His mum called him Hilarion, but he hated that name.

– Why?

– Why did she call him that, or why did he hate the name?

– Both.

Sometimes she says, Both; sometimes she says, I know why he hated his name. The story I can tell almost by rote, but she likes to vary her contributions.

– I don't know why she chose Hilarion. Maybe it was her way of railing at Fate.

– *Railing* at Fate.

She sounds satisfied with the phrase.

– Because it wasn't *hilarious*.

That was Josh's joke originally.

– Well, you know how it starts: We once lived with an

extraordinarily ugly child who wasn't ugly at all and who loved –

– Every moment, even the last one.

– And who was a friend of butterflies.

– Yes! – and she adds, as she always has – That was really true?

– Well, butterflies certainly came to him. He'd be sitting or lying somewhere round the house and all of a sudden, there's a butterfly. Your mum said three had come on different days into the ward while she was there. They'd perch on his hand or forehead and then fly away again.

– Josh says it was because, you know, he dribbled.

– That's possible. I wonder though. The place where his nose wasn't, that was always damp, but I never saw a butterfly land there.

– Just being comforting. Just being real friends.

– Yes, real as us sitting here. As real as the sun.

– As real as Josh fishing. As real as those mayflies.

– No, they're fungus gnats.

– Ooo yuck. I like mayflies better.

– Ah but these gnats dance better.

– Like they're on little rubber bands. Invisible ones.

– Mmm, does look like that. They're lekking.

– So Ari looked really really ugly.

– Well, you couldn't tell that because he almost always wore a mask, a light white ceramic mask that went from his eyebrows to –

– With only one eye looking out and a hole in the chin for the dribble.

– Under the chin. He could only use one eye because the other one was dead.

– Did it look dead?

– Are you making a pun?

– No, asking.

– Yes, it did. Kind of withered in the socket. It should've been replaced by a nice glass one when he was little, but that never happened.

– Because his mum hid him away and then she died and then he was sick and then he was dying.

– In brief, that's it.

– And then my mum helped him.

– She asked Josh and me first, would we mind if she brought some work home. It was very nice work she said, careful and gentle and polite, and it wouldn't be for long.

– Why did she say careful and polite?

– Well because she had brought home another person from the hospice section –

– Hoss pissss not hoss spit all –

– Indeed. But that person had been rude and mostly very drunken and he'd frightened Josh.

– Did he die too?

– Yes. Back in the hospice though. Your mum gave him a break so he could go in his wheelchair to the races one last time, and have tea with a real family one last time.

– Was I here then?

– No, Josh was only seven then.

– I'll be eight soon.

– Don't I know it. And look at Josh, big gangly bugger.

– That's rude.

– Only a little bit. I mean it affectionately. Anyway, she brought Ari home because he was young and distressed by the other dying people. It was her holidays and he didn't have any visitors.

– Why?

– He didn't have any family. The other kids he'd known in the hospital had gone home or –

– What does Hilarion mean?

– I'm not sure. I think it might be related to Hilary, which means cheerful.

– Like 'Josh' means 'Joshua' really.

– Maybe.

– And my name means 'good and fortunate'.

– Even so.

– And Flann means 'a boy with red hair'.

She giggles.

I am Flann. My hair is grey.

– Say the hair bit. The whole bit.

– When you very little, we once lived with an extraordinarily ugly child who wasn't ugly at all. He loved every moment he lived, even the last one, and butterflies befriended him. But he was ugly beyond belief if you only looked at his face ... from the back he looked normal, even beautiful, a slender, straight-limbed boy with delicate hands. His hair was black and so silky fine that, if he turned his head suddenly, it would float a second before settling.

– Ahhh.

She stands suddenly.

– Josh has got a fish!

– Good. Fresh searun trout for our supper.

– No, he's putting it back.

– Why ever did I introduce him to the concept of catch and release?

– You're teasing aren't you?

– A bit.

– Ari didn't eat things did he?

– Not things you had to chew. Just soups. Shakes. Juices. The hospice gave your mum special feeding things.

– And Ari comes home with Mum, and he shakes your hand and Josh's hand and says, Hello –

– in a very slushy way because his teeth went every which way and his lips weren't properly formed –

– and his mouth went right round one side.

– Well, halfway across his left cheek.

– And you know because he took off his mask for you.

– Yes, and as you know, Josh did something marvellous. He stared for a minute in silence then said, Mum says you like butterflies? Ari says, Yes – it sounds like Lessh. And Josh says, Well hello and here's a butterfly kiss, and made one on his good cheek. And we all laughed.

– I love Josh.

– You and me both.

– But why did he take off the mask?

– It was a gift. Without words, he said, This is me. You should know what I look like before you get to know who I am.

– But he didn't say that. You said that.

– That is my job after all. Helping people with words. Sharing and teaching words.

– Did you teach Ari?

– He was mainly too tired to learn. He spoke good English too, once you learned his pronunciation. Besides, in a way he was teaching us. Even when he just lay on the sofa. There was one day I took him to look at the garden and he became entranced by the potato flowers. I don't think he'd seen them before. I'd seen thousands, but I only learned to truly see them by watching Ari touch one and say how beautiful the yellow cup was, how it rested on the cream star. He'd look at things so intensely. Or do whatever needed doing, wiping away his saliva say, as though that was the only thing that mattered.

Until the next moment came along and then that'd get his wholehearted attention. And he found a quiet joy in most moments. He endured what he had to and enjoyed the rest. I don't know whether he did that because he knew he was dying, or because that was the way he innately was. We only had three weeks of him.

– I know you say you and Mum learned then that the only moment is now. I know that's what you say. I just don't know what it means.

– What it says. I find it hard too, o most wonderful daughter in all the world.

She has Marie's grace as well as her name. She doesn't simper. She accepts.

– You see, we can live in our memories or live in our hopes and fears. Or, we can live in this moment, you and me, talking, the sun there, the river here, and Josh somewhere round the bend –

– He's over under the kānukas.

– remembering another time and other people, for sure, but also hearing the ripples rippling like a plenum of giggles, and watching the lekking flies.

She has Marie's beautiful deep-brown eyes too. They're fixed on my face as she ignores my trailed teaching opportunities.

– Because it's the only time we can be sure of, the only time we really have. Now.

– You miss Mum don't you.

– All the time.

– Was she there when Ari died?

– Yes. She was holding him, and I was holding Josh. He had his head buried in my shoulder. We were outside because Ari had whispered, Sun. Marie had taken his mask off for him, and he lay in her arms feeling the sun on his bare face. And all I could think to do was murmur his poem again and again.

– Say the poem.

Pleases and thankyous are words she almost never uses. Her smiles do the job instead.

– He who binds to himself a joy
Doth the winged life destroy;
But he who kisses the joy as it flies
Lives in Eternitys sun rise.

– Did you write that for him?

– No. It's by a marvellous mystical word magician called William Blake.

– Why is it Ari's then?

– I thought I had told you this before?

– Yes, but it's part of the story my dad.

– Because it was on the potato flower day. I'd picked a flowerhead to take inside for him. He didn't exactly protest my action, just said, when he was back on the couch, I can still see it inside my head when I want. It did look good with the green leaves. And I thought, Ah that is Blake to the core, and quoted the stanza to him.

– Did he hear you? That other day I mean?

– I don't know. He didn't react to anything really by then. Except – well, his breathing started to falter, not harshly, it just took a little longer each time between breaths.

– And the butterflies came.

– Six of them from nowhere, little tussock blues.

– And Josh looked.

– I don't know what made him do that. He just decided to lift his head.

– And he said, Butterfly kisses.

– Yes. And Ari must have heard him because he opened his eye and we think he smiled.

– And that was when –

– he stopped breathing. Just like that. That quiet, that peaceful.

– Josh remembers the butterflies. I'm going to go and ask him something.

– Okay.

It really was probably the moisture that brought the butterflies – they come to carrion and puddles after all – but I don't know. I don't remember seeing them go. And I remember the potato flowers, and the yellow admiral that winged onto them and settled for long minutes while the boy savoured it with a bright crooked eye, and Marie's grin. Some people have birds, she said, but he has even more beautiful messengers.

She should have had a phoenix, aflame with a compassion like her own, or a tintinnabulation of bellbirds – that 'most tuneable silver sound' – as herald and signal. Instead of the squeal of brakes –

But I'm still here with my growing children, Josh showing Marie the best place to cast, and I can feel the sun too, and am, despite it all, happy to sit in this present moment watching – pax, desire to always name things correctly –

watching the mayflies dance.

The Trouble with A. Chen Li

THE MISTAKE I MADE
was simple, understandable.
I didn't think he could follow me.
The distance gauge on the ride read 1006 miles. He'd made it in nine days.

He is sprawled outside the tent, worn nearly to unconsciousness with exhaustion.

His half-open eyes look into mine and what he sees there doesn't give him comfort. The eyelids drag shut on tears.

Picking him up isn't easy. Not that he's heavy, just awkward to hold. His head and torso are those of an eight year old but the rest of him – isn't.

There's no sand-nest in the tent of course, so I arrange him on the floor, and wrap my blanket round his shoulders. His limbs twitch and quiver. Eventually, he sleeps.

◆◆◆

When Chen arches his legs and stands on tiptoe, he reaches my shoulder, but walking normally has him at waist level. I know he can jump over my head from a standing start. I've seen him swarm with elegant ease straight up a tree or the side of a cliff, and he can move astonishingly fast.

I just didn't realise he was capable of very long distance running. Or that he had the endurance – and the need – to follow me across the Hohum Plains, and catch up with me so fast.

Well, it's not the first time I've underestimated him.

It probably won't be the last.

And I've had just three days of peace –

◆◆◆

I fell into this place, I think.

I remember standing, confused, cold, fearful, in the bus shelter. It was growing dark and I was worried the buses might have ceased running altogether. I was afraid a slash gang might come by although this was supposed to be safe area. I was tired too.

These fears and discomforts weren't unusual however, and I should remember what happened next. I have tried my best to remember. All I can recall is an overwhelming crashing sound and total dark and a sensation of falling forever.

I didn't land anywhere. The crashing sound faded. The dark lightened by imperceptible degrees until I could see greyness, and then feel I was lying on something soft yet smooth.

The first surprise was that I could see. Clearly, exactly. I haven't ever been able to do that, except very occasionally with the aid of an ocular, and then only when I focused on something still and small, like a coin or a fragment of pottery or delicately flaked blade.

The second surprise was the way I felt.

I felt happy. I felt supple and healthy and alert. I was relaxed and painfree. I might have felt like this as a child but my childhood was sixty years distant and I have forgotten it.

And then the Voice sounded inside my head.

'Hello,' it said.

I was comforted by the banality. I had just had a suspicion I might be dead.

Obviously not.

'In a minute, the door will open. Outside is your ride. We have selected food and drinks you will enjoy for your cupboard, and your tent contains all you will need for a basic but comfortable life. There is an information source in the cupboard and in emergencies, you can contact me.'

'Where am –'

'Goodbye.'

Arabic numerals were flashing in the grey 47…46…45… 44…

They are shining cerulean, perfectly clear 23…22…21...

The 0 fades into an iris-style door: it opens. Outside is sky, pale blue and streaked with distant cirrus.

Whatever I am lying on has shrunk away. The greyness is rolling into itself. It vanishes without fuss or sound. The grass under my rump is short and wiry. And cold. Naturally, I stand, just like that, straight up. That's when I discover some very surprising things indeed. About me.

◆◆◆

This story is about Chen. How I met Chen. What happened next. So, cupboards and rides and tents and books won't be explained. The words mean something like I thought they would when I heard them, indeed they do. I shelter in the tent. The ride will transport me over land and water at the rate of 200 miles a day – but it is windy and not exactly comfortable to travel on. The cupboard does contain foods and drinks I enjoy, and much else besides, but I would give my soul – if such exists – for one litre of good claret and almost any kind of food that had once bled. Don't pass me the tripe and the brains, but o (moan) for a garlic and black peppered steak! Crayfish! Chicken Kiev! Oysters! Tuna sashimi!

I have wasted so much time composing meals, so very much. And my salivary glands ache –

Chen. I fell into his place too. Literally.

◆◆◆

The ride had been designed for a narrower arse than mine, and for some being with longer arms, but it was great fun to play with, at first. It could trundle along at walking pace or you could really wind it up and hit 60 70 miles an hour (the designers had a sense of whimsy: the speedo showed everything from leagues to muang, as did the distance gauge, but I settled on miles). I'm your average human ape in many ways so I played with it. I hooned over grass and the low anomalous shrubbery. I learned to swing the thing in a tight figure-of-eight and sling the thing fast as (78.832 mph) at the only landmark nearby and swerve over it by round past –

It had something like – gyroscopic inertial control? It took a good deal of slinging and flinging and swinging to actually tip the ride to any kind of spill point. It was clearly designed, I decided after an hour or so of happy playing, for sedate conformists who wished to trundle from point a to point b, quietly.

For there was no noisy exhaust or reverberating motor or yowl of acceleration. Silently, with the faintest of sprays (water, as far as I could determine) the ride would accelerate at my thumb pressure on the left handlebar, lift according to contour of land or water underneath – never higher than a metre – and sough away. Any noise as you hit 78.832 mph was windrush past your own outsticking ears, echoes in the hollows of your head.

◆◆◆

If I swerved violently, it would keel over but there was – *if we encounter technology beyond the reach of our imagination, we will think it magic.*

I am very quickly bored although I have learned, over the years, to stifle the screams of rage a raw primate might vent, unconstrained. It took me a mere hour to explore the wonders of sight (it will take me a lifetime to appreciate – as no-one except the nearly blind can – the wonders of sight). It took me a day to explore the ride and realise that, no matter what I did – drive straight at the rocks, lurch over until I was nearly parallel with the grass, scream round in tight circles and suddenly turn out of them – I could not hurt myself. There seemed to be an invisible impalpable – membrane? protecting me. Which meant, as rider, I could nearly crash into things and nearly have what looks and touches like a piece of heavy machinery, dark grey and metallic (but it could be protoplasm for all I know), fall on me – but such accidents wouldn't happen.

While I was on the ride.

◆◆◆

After I recovered from the surprise of learning how I'd been – rearranged, I did take note of the surroundings. In my early days, I had sufficient vision to learn horizons, depth perception, three dimensionality, so the clarity of sight I had now wasn't confusing. The landscape was rather limited for enjoyment however.

Where I first stood was a small grassy amphitheatre, twenty maybe thirty metres across. One third of the perimeter – to my left as I stood there first – was a roiling endless wall of nasty rainbows. A very stupid being would take one look – or sniff – at it and back away fast. I am not stupid. I turned and ran up to the right lip of the amphitheatre. When I swung around – heart not even thumping but eyes wide (I had never *felt* my eyes go wide before – I mean, that would not be a sensible thing for my eyes to do) I nearly banged into the ride.

The membrane effect: I couldn't bang into it. There it was, a dark metre long, narrow saddle, pannier bags behind (tent and cupboard and book as I later learned). And – five thousand years of horse-lords and camel riders and ass-bestriders not to mention Free Sailors came whipping out of the gene pool and said, Control this and go where you will –

basic control was sitting on the thing and holding the handlebar. It smoothed along slowly, doing what I wanted, getting away from the rainbow wall.

Outside of the amphitheatre was grass. Low grass. An almost featureless seemingly endless grass plain.

Imagine a paddock that has been cropped for millennia by,

say, sheep? There is only grass in the paddock. The nutrient levels have been kept up, the soil structure maintained, and any other grass-eating pest exterminated. But the grass has grown tired, in some deep unspeakable way, of being cropped. It has grown tired of being grass.

That is what this stuff looked like. Nearly-dead. Lacklustre. Unlively.

The only other thing visible was a rockstack. It stood like a solitary finger against the horizon.

The distance gauge read 17 miles when I stopped by it. The stack appeared to be made of fractured grey ignimbrite. Nothing grew on it, that I could see but I couldn't see round it. Maybe there was something, even someone, on the other side...

I slide cautiously off the ride and wonder, for the first time, O, do I need clothes round here?

– Do you know I've never seen myself naked that I can recall? Partly limited eyesight, but partly because I disliked what my body must look like – plump, shortlimbed, almost seal-like, on a par with my face which was round and chinless. So I never looked in mirrors and learned from my parents' disgust with me to despise my epicene form. Fat useless poof was the kindest term my father used. When I showered, I wrapped a towel around my waist. My most glamorous clothes were my thick flannel pyjamas.

O do I need clothes round here?

It's not only my body that has been altered: something has played round with my mind as well.

I walked round the rockstack but it was bare rockstack all round. The tired grass lay limply about it. Ahead was more tired grass, leagues of it, and then an encompassing wall of grey mist. I walked back round and sat down, back leant against the rock so I wouldn't have to look over the dreariness.

And – very suddenly – the weirdness of it all caught up with me. *Where am I? What has happened? I've lost the Special Library books. Where are they? Who will feed Ympenchka – he'll be getting hungry by now and yowling for me and nextdoor hates that and –*

and at the thought of his soft cream fur and rough little tongue, his throbbing purr, I started sobbing. The joy of feeling healthy and changed to perfection suddenly ebbed to utter tiredness, aloneness, bereftness, and I truly felt like dying.

'Open me.'

It was the left pannier.

This did not surprise. I didn't care about anything any more. But the pannier was persistent.

'Open me,' it kept fluting at ten-second intervals until I leapt up and grabbed at it. My touch – I've since learned – was enough. The pannier opened and unfolded and became a three-metre tube tent that snaked over me and the ride. Over half the instant floor raised itself and looked invitingly soft … the other pannier produced a large blanket, made of a material like grey silk velvet, and I curled up in that, curled up on the mattressy floor, and fell deeply asleep.

◆◆◆

Well, I learned what the cupboard contained – pleasant sober vegetable food and drink – and how to use the book which was something like a computer and something like an interface with my own brain, and I travelled for twenty days over the grass plains. I had discovered the compass dial on the ride. I was heading west.

I missed my cat more and more. I began to miss people though I met few enough – the librarian of the talking books section; the social welfare worker who called once every six months, the museum curator who would permit me to observe an object, and the very occasional client who wanted to commission a work. I even caught myself waxing nostalgic for my vile-tongued neighbours, who kept three Rottweilers and had more than once threatened to sic them on Ympie or me.

There was the grass plain, and an occasional rockstack. I stopped at each one and examined them but never saw so much as a beetle. No birds flew through the sky. There were no bushes, no trees. The weather became mist at the horizon every evening, and fine at every dawn. Except there didn't seem to be a sun, just a darkening of the sky which lightened unknown hours later.

◆◆◆

I had stopped the ride when the light was at its height. I pretended it was noon, was lunchtime.

Today, let us have the brown rice cakes with tomato salsa and some green things that could be beans.

Tasty enough but some rich pork sausages, with crackly brown skins and little white studs of delicious …

someone is singing. Someone is singing nearby.

It is a slightly hoarse voice and very definitely off key, but it is quite loud.

I don't think I have started hearing things but I can *not* understand this!

Ringaring a rosies

a pocket full a posies.

I am creeping towards the voice and I feel my hair standing on end

a tissue a tissue

and I fall through the grass

◆◆◆

A child face, flushed, and dark slanted eyes glittering with excitement –

'I thought you were dead!' it exclaims happily.

'Oowww,' is all I can manage. There's a plum-sized bump on my right temple and my neck and shoulder feel wrenched. Yet, even as I tentatively move them, the pain lessens, and the lump under my fingers diminishes. So I sit up.

The excited little face is two metres away. It peers over an odd furry palisade. The palisade seems part of a sandheap, and I'm sitting on soft dry sand. Above me is a gaping hole where I ripped through grass and roots, and behind me – turning towards another sound I never thought I'd miss – a tiny stream runs down a course in a steepsided gully. A whole other landscape under the grass ...

'Are you alright?' and just as I notice the child's hair is an extraordinary rose-pink shade, and factor in that the top of the palisade is the same colour, the palisade spreads and flattens and angles, is suddenly revealed as giant arachnoid legs, with a human torso freakishly perched on top of a goldenfurred thorax.

Something stops me from screaming, but my eyes seem to have swollen nearly out of their sockets. I have stood, fists clenched, before I'm aware of doing it.

The gaudy head tilts: the child-thing looks up at me with a wide white-toothed grin.

'Nah, you look alright. I gotta real surprise! You want something to eat? I gotta hamburgher and a shake. You can have them? There's the water too but it tastes funny. No birds around now. I can get you one later though. Umm, can you talk? Do you just make sounds?'

'Who ... are you?' I am proud, afterwards, that I didn't say What.

'O I'm Chen. Chen Li. A. Chen Li.'

Old habits of courtesy kick in.

'Pleased to meet you, Chen.' Drawing a deep breath. 'Albeit an unexpected pleasure. I'm Oliver Marsh. Well, I was Oliver Marsh. I'm not sure who I am now,' holding out my hand.

The – Chen giggles and shakes it. The hand feels perfectly normal.

'You talk like a perfesser! Do I say Oliver or Perfesser?' and giggle becomes snigger.

gods, how I grew to hate that snigger

'Oliver. Never Olly.'

'Okay. Wanna burgher?'

◆◆◆

The burger: think, Macfood. Goodness knows what went into beef hamburgers when the world ran (we thought) normally, twentieth century style gross.

Scrotums, lips, anal muscles we knew about and ignored as best we could but there were also additives and supplements and enhancements which could have been anything, and were.

I had been wanting food-that-bled so hard for less than a moon, and what I got was congealed ersatz tasteless cheese on top of dubious carbonised sundries, which, charitably, might have been meat. And ketchup. And white hydrogenated bread. And the shake Chen generously gave me? (he is generous within his tiny ambit). Think artificiality from glycerine thickener to GE soy. A real cow's teat never got near the milk.

◆◆◆

'What did you choose?' asks Chen.

'I didn't choose. I was never offered a choice. I think They looked into my head and saw I loved animals and decided only vegetable food was suitable, good, for me. And you?'

'Welll … I din know much, I loved the hamburgher and shake my gran brought. I wanted that.'

'So you got that?'

'Yep! An I can eat as much as I *want*! Drink as much as an I do! It never runs out!'

'And never changes?'

'Nope.' A long silence. 'I'm kinda sick of it.'

◆◆◆

This I have gathered:

Chen lived in Auckland somewhere.

He thought his mum was Chinese. Her thought his gran was not. 'Sheuz brown like me but her eyes were different.' Dad? Uncles? Grandfather? Forget them, they weren't there.

He – we established early on he was male. ('Ooo waaayyy, I never seen one that long!' 'How many have you seen?' 'Welll, only mine…'

That's all I've ever seen too.)

And that he'd never been to school: television was his school, and people a rarity in his life.

There had been something wrong with his legs: he can't ever remember walking then.

'And then they started to rot. Man, they *stank*. Made me feel really sick.'

One day, the television died. The room light wouldn't work. The heater stopped. He remembers the room, the room both he and his mother lived and slept in, and his gran when she came, the room growing dark and very cold.

'Then I woke up here! I remember asking for the burgher and shake and that I could walk.' He puffed out his chest and proudly surveys his array of limbs.

'Man, can I walk or what!' and he dances past me, eight legs and two – things at the front by the mandibles?

– Pedipalps, advises the Book, the back ones are spinnerets – and his arms undulate gracefully, and he skitters down the creek.

◆◆◆

It would've been at least three months later, if we had a moon. Light periods are difficult to keep track of as sometimes I'll curl up my blanket and tent and emerge when I feel ready with no idea of what time has passed. The Book labels my entries and queries in simple numerical order.

Chen sleeps like that too. He has three other sand-nests aside from the one I fell into. One is twenty miles distant, where the bird flock is. 'Bird', I suppose, is the best name for them. They look like nearly beakless penguin chicks, fat shuffling grey-downy blobs with small dim eyes. They honk in a pained way except when Chen leaps on one and his mandibles go to work. Then the flock – sighs.

He brought one back for me.

'But I don't eat meat raw. Or juicify and suck it or whatever it is you do.'

'No worries Ol'! I gotta fire.'

He chattered on about seeing this TV movie and this sidsloth thing that had scratched rocks together and made fire and he'd hunted round for rocks ('a long time, a really long time man') scratching and banging them together until he found some ('on that rockthing over there' gesturing vaguely south) that made sparks and – by long trial and error I assume, discovered how to ignite grass, and in turn, set fire to an oil shale he discovered in one of the caverns. Once the shale was set on fire, it didn't go out.

At that cavern (where Chen has built another heapedup sand-nest) while waiting for the clay-wrapped bird to finish cooking, I ask

'Why did you go looking for rocks to make fire?'

He shrugs.

'Warm. Thought it'd be sorta company?'

I wonder how long Chen has been in this – place.

'Now I got you!'

The birdthing tasted foul, sour and viscous, with tiny pinfeathers studded through its skin.

◆◆◆

Three months, roughly: we'd explored all Chen had already discovered (the three caverns, all of them topped by rockstacks, and two with underground gigantic trees (Chen, at my request, checked their bare gray trunks, the limp feathery tops for 'Beetles, anything,' I asked. 'Nothin anywhere,' he answered); the bird flock; the stream that appeared to have no life in it except water, and which started in one of the caverns and disappeared into a seep when the gully ended in a granite-looking wall).

I'd taken to pitching the tent (quaint usage when your tent unfurls itself and will produce an entrance or window wherever you decide you want one) further and further away from Chen. For one thing, he'd start his raucous attempts at singing whenever he felt like it.

'You like songs Ol'? Man I love Che Fu on TV! I love that! Can't do that though but I know whasstuff Gran showed me. You know 'Piku Toro'?'
and before I can say anything he launches into it. And 'One Day A Taniha' and 'There Was An Ol Womim Who Swallow A Fly' and 'He Putiputi' and 'Bla Baa Back Sheep' and every other mispronounced and otherwise verbally mangled

kiddysong he's learned.

I don't remember learning nursery rhymes.

But he'd run that same question and scenario and songfest every second day it seemed.

I tried to explain.

My idea of heaven was a bottle of claret or merlot, Ympenchka on my lap, and, say, the Toccata and Fugue, over an hour of ascending glory, or something tinkly but logical, Scarlatti for instance, early Vivaldi. The only times I felt as happy was when a client had specified the object (for some reason, the Matakana sawedged flint stays in mind) and paid me to produce one of my strange drawings – hyperdetailed for the first sixty degrees but sliding into sfumato and nothingness as your eye edged around the circle.

I think my cat is dead.

Well, I know I am never going to see him again.

◆◆◆

It was probably just a quarter of a year, when I heard one snigger too many, one tuneless song grating my ears to much, one overwhelming episode of nosepicking or armpit farting or another eight year old's grossness, and snarled,

'You are truly loathsome. I hate you. Go away.'

And Chen looked at me, slightly hurt, obviously wondering what loathsome meant, and asked

'Where to Ol'?'

◆◆◆

So, roughly three months later: I had realised that I healed extremely quickly now. It wasn't only the bump on the head and the wrenched shoulder. I tried sticking a sharp flake of stone into a wrist vein. It spurted, hurt, and sealed. The cut was gone before dark. There was never any scar.

Chen had mentioned that he had burned part of one leg when he set the shale on fire ('It was okay the next day,' shrugging).

And I had had time to put it all together.

There weren't wonders in this place.

There weren't real satisfactions in this place.

Nothing will change.

Chen won't – couldn't – become other than the age he was. He might obtain new memories, new experiences, but they wouldn't mature him. He was trapped in eightness as I was trapped in three score and ten.

Nothing can change.

There were two incompatibles who, through neither's fault, would never grow close.

Two incompatibles who probably couldn't be killed.

But I was getting to the stage where I was going to try. Murder. Suicide.

So, while Chen slept – and snored – I climbed aboard the ride and headed away.

Now, as he twitches in his tiredness, forlornness, I realise we are Something Else's game.

And I know a name for this place.

Incubation

HE LOOKED like a two year old but his body was sixteen. His mind hadn't achieved continence yet let alone language. And he might have been – o, maybe –

I was in the Far North, it had been a ruggedly emotional takiauē, and the day was fiercely hot: heat waves danced off the bitumen, and the airconditioning and the fan weren't even drying my sweat let alone cooling the hover van.

Ahead was a caravan, a patch of scrub, a large scrawled sign: MĒRANA.

Think pink lush sweetness, think juice, think cool cool drink.

Also, think potheads, squalor, rabid dogs – but already I was pulling over. The juice and cool won.

The scrub crackled and fizzed with a million cicadas: there was a large garden meandering by its southern edge. I put on my sunguard and poncho and stepped down from the van.

The caravan had a wide awning and in its shade a barebottomed infant squatted, industriously patting mud into pies. It ignored me. There didn't sound to be any dogs, anybody else, and I couldn't see a melon anywhere.

'Kia ora?'

There was a squeaking from behind the caravan and a man pushing a barrow came out.

'Yeah cheers mate – they're ten dollar each.' He grins proudly, as well he might.

Celadon globes, big as soccer balls, with wide intenselygreen stripes, fill the barrow.

'Holy!' I pick up one and it is heavy, dense with promise. It knocks right too.

'You religious?'

'Nah.'

'Me neither.' Which is a bit odd: his rustyblack hair is in full dreads with what looks like real turquoise and coral beads bound onto some locks. That shouts Neorasta these days.

'So you'll go a melon?'

'You bet. Three please.' Which is all the change I've got.

'Like me to slice a bit of one?'

'Oh yes,' and then I think, Whoops, him getting a knife out might not be a good idea, but as I offer him the first melon and pick out another couple and lay them carefully by the barrow wheel, he takes out a small folder and deftly carves out a perfect pink smile and hands it back to me. It beads with pale dew: it is perfectly ripe and cool as autumn water.

'Good eh? I keep 'em in a shadepit round the back. 'Nother slice?'

Mmm I say thickly, mouth full and dribbling a bit.

The relentless glare of the sun seems to have calmed down a degree. And while I eat that, he knots a carrier for each fruit, complete with handles, swiftly and precisely out of flax strips.

'Done that fairly often?'

'I reckon.' He places the cut melon, slash side upwards, in

the last carrier. 'Sell about fifty sixty when it's this kind of day. About a hundred of this kind of day these years.'

'*Lot* of melons.'

'Well, that's my thing. Make compost, start out the seedlings, grow melons, sell melons. Eat 'em too.' He has a wide white grin. It makes his face light despite the browridges and heavy rounded jaw.

I glance over to the rambling garden. I can't see anything like melon vines.

He's quick. He catches the glance.

'You wanna hear a little story? Won't take long and I'll make you cuppa green tea too. Best thing for the heat, melon and green tea,' and his look at me is sharp, but not unkind.

Pink people like me wearing sunguards and sunponchos aren't common in the Far North. We die of heatstroke with quick and surprising ease. It has to be a serious matter to bring us to this end of the island and I would bet he has already spotted the Tahu logo on the van, put two and two together and come up with grief.

The shade under the awning is much cooler than I would have thought. The caravan door is open and rather than dogstink squalor, the room inside is clean and almost bare. Builtin doublebunk one end: gas hob and sink and cupboards the other, and nothing in between.

The infant goes on making its mudpies. They are clumsy misshapen discs. There is something strange, unfinishedlooking, about its face. It ignores us both, even when the man gently pats its head.

There is a foldup table and chairs leaning against one side of the awning. The man sets them up in his quick and dexterous way, brings out a white porcelain pot and two cups a moment later.

The tea is as refreshing as the melon slices.

He says, no bytalk or preliminary, 'Twenty years ago I lived in Auckland. Was a DJ, made good money, believed all my heart in God, smoked sweet loads and met lotta women. One – well, she was the one. We were family for nearly three years.' He nods to the busy child. 'He came along in the third year and she split ten months later.'

That's shocking. Not the woman abandoning her kid – but that something that looks – oh, two? – is much older. When I look back at the man, he grins.

'No-one knows why. He grew to that size then stopped. They reckon his mind stopped growing before he got to be a year, well before. She knew that. She'd had a baby before. This one was – wrong. I don't blame her. I'm used to him but I didn't carry him, suckle him. Just look after whatever he needs, either end. Bit of food, bit of water … that's all he does.'

The infant lays another lopsided pie on the nearest teetery pile.

'Can make hundreds in a day. Never seems to notice that I scrape 'em up in the evening and make 'em back into a heap for the next day.' The grin is gone.

'Had to leave the city. One thing, he screamed all the time. 'Nother thing, other kids would really boot into him.

Wasn't safe for him to be with anyone else. So, traipsed round caravan parks, living on the benefit, getting shoved out when the complaints about the noise got too many. Getting really pissed off with the system too. Nobody knew anything, could suggest any help.'

He refills our cups. 'Grow this too … nobody helped except one of my aunties. She said, Come back to this bit of land I've got. There's a stream, good earth. You can park your van there and he'll have a bit of space. Maybe that's what he needs, not all this noise and rush. Well, he stopped screaming that's for sure. And as soon as he felt this loam underfoot he touched it like I never saw him touch anything before. And that's when he started the production line. Me, I grew a bit of dope, sold a bit. But the pleasure had gone out of it. I thought, Shit, here I am, not yet twenty-five, no joy from the responsibility, no hope. No god any more – couldn't believe in any god after he came along.'

'I know this'll sound callous but couldn't you have um –'

'Dumped him in some kind of residential care? Isn't any for ones like him. Dumped him fullstop? Thought about it many times. Every time I did, he'd smile, big unwitting grin. The only time he does it. Thought about offing him too. That's when he uses his only word. Dudduddud. Scary or what? Figured I'm stuck with him as long as he lasts. It's okay now, no real trouble and hey, I got my melon farm.'

'Which isn't the garden over there.'

'Nah, that's just veg for us. The chooks are in the scrub, and the tea shrubs. And the melonry.'

'Love the word.'

'Yeah, good eh? Auntie got us started. Gave us a broody chook and her eggs. Gave us a peach tree from her garden, corn seed, the old style potatoes, kūmara, beans. Told us about composting. Wāta kirihi in the stream. Tuna and kōura too, but we don't eat flesh we have to kill. That's just my thing – Auntie raised chooks for tucker, and pigs. And she gave us a watermelon one scorcher of a day. Don't let him eat the seeds she warned but he got some anyway. She died a week later. About a year later I knew he'd eaten seeds cause I found where he'd crapped and there's these three great coiling green vines with about a hundred baby melons on 'em. And they grew, o how they grew. Sold half for a couple of hundred. Thought, Hmmm. Figured I better feed 'em and organise 'em a bit. Trouble was, only stuff I could find about growing lotsa melon was for big farms. Agribiz. Told us about chemical fertilisers and hectarage and sprays and trellising. Not my league. And I *knew* I was onto a good natural thing if I could work out how to grow enough here … good natural heh.' He has an abrupt laugh, like a yelp. 'Still a bit of that old jah stuff in me.'

'Noticed the hair,' I say, deadpan.

'Hey, don't knock it. Costs nothing, good as a sunguard and keeps you warm in winter!'

'Can't argue with that.'

'Anyway, one morning I'm hugging my head, must be a way, must be a way, and I noticed something odd. He's patted the pie pile into a sort of mound and just wandered off to sit with the chooks. They like him. They come lay their eggs here by the door when he's not making pies and croon at him. Last cuppa?'

'Yeah please.'

'It all sort of tumbled together. Mounds like kūmara mounds but big mothers made of compost. Make 'em in the shelter of the bush. Chooks'll do the job on the insect pests. All I'll have to do is weed at the start and carry water.

◆◆◆

It's a sight to see, the melonry. Thirty waisthigh mounds, a vine flourishing all over each one, and a neat circle of stone slabs round the base.

There's a small double-bay compost bin to one side. And just as I'm thinking, Wonder how that can provide enough fertility? he says, 'Yeah, well, we don't produce much green waste the two of us. Not even if you add all the chook dung. There's only fifteen of them. Mounds are mostly beach sand with a bit of loam.'

'So you use ah bush stuff?'

'Nah. One mudpie apiece is all it seems to take.'

He swung his dreads back over his shoulders.

'Mind you, they're the *special* pies.'

Question me, the *special* said.

'Not the production line model I take it?'

'Sometimes, sometimes …'

he draws circles with his left big toe in the dusty ground

'he'll get, not frantic but, but, speedily oh – deliberate?

And I'll follow him down to the beach and he'll pick up one crab shell after another, taste this bit of dried kelp and reject it for dried bladder wrack and then pick up a feather, ordinary gull's feather and sniff and sniff and throw it away and pick up a nondescript one beside it.'

He sighs. 'That one I knew was a godwit pinion.'

Really good eyesight. Really good observer.

'And trotting back here, he'll –'

He rubbed his nose and shook his head. The coral and turquoise and jade clinked –

'I shouldn't say he. Got all the bits for both and more. But I'm used to thinking him, he – so. Anyway, he'll put the beach findings in and he'll pat and hum and taste occasionally and add odd other things, ashes, leaves, pebbles, and eventually he'll make a way bigger firmer pie than usual.'

A little silence.

'And that one?' I suggest.

'I stick in a mound.' He has a lovely loud-toothed grin. 'He does stuff with the seeds too. I gotta bag of saved seeds and he'll play with handfuls and wind up with one that suits him, suits his pie.'

'Which you plant?'

'You bet! I haven't been stupid enough to experiment.' He sniffed. 'I think he does. If a retard can experiment. C'mn look at this.'

At the back of the melonry, in the mānuka shade, is a smaller mound. The foliage is subdued, and the small melon is a breathtaking redbrown in colour.

'Gonna be interesting to taste that one eh?'

'I'd think so.'

'Mind you, one came up last year that was black and white. Zebra stripes. Had no flesh, just a heap of seeds inside. Really choice, roasted.'

Back at the caravan, the infant is still making pies.

Or rather, a pie. It is the size of a saucer and has a flattened rim. A chook sits on narrow infant shoulders, wings downspread. A living cloak.

And suddenly the blighted child lifts its head and stares at me.

It is like being stared at by two halogen lamps.

The gaze is so intense I don't note the colour of its eyes.

The chook eyes are way more empathetic.

It gives the pie a final pat. I notice a small brown seed flattened down, vanished under the mud.

'Well now,' says the melon seller, 'I'll take that to your van too?'

◆◆◆

I travelled back home. I put the mudpie in a bonsai pot and judiciously watered it. Nothing happened throughout our southern winter but in late spring –

surprise! A mānuka sprout. And over the months, it grew – not into a wispy spire or straggle-bush, but a kānuka-like miniature tree. Last week there were buds. Tonight, they have opened.

Wonderful bright blue flowers with a scent of melons –

and pushing through the soil now, the tiniest greenest stick insect I have ever seen –

it teeters towards the strange mānuka

it sways on one narrow limb

it stills

o, and I have a suspicion that when the flowers turn to seed capsules, they will have unusual virtues. I will not be surprised if the stick insect behaves peculiarly either. I plan to take them everywhere I go. And we'll see

– o, maybe, was a godlet?

Midden Mine

STARING INTO THE PIT,
thinking
Has to be a fraud, has to be. But who would do it? Bea? Pigs can fly ... Ellen? Nah, too keen on the received wisdom and besides, it wouldn't do her career any good whatsoever. Cameron? He's a possibility but I would've thought he'd have been way too drunk to walk out here let alone plant the thing so skilfully. The undergrads? Fond of hoaxing and we were talking ooparts the first night they arrived. But this was an undisturbed section.

And I uncovered it.

A dark night and seafog thickening.

I think
all we find
is what we're looking for

Hmm. Sometimes her words worked, and sometimes they seemed to miss the boat entirely. Then I'd think about them again.

The oystercatchers are crying Keria keria! so a storm is coming despite this languid fog. Replace the tarpaulin and head for bed. Tomorrow is another year.

End of the Month

I'm to have the next day entirely to myself, which will be a grand opportunity to wander around, and get a feel for the place. The geo types have left an excellent set of maps, hard copies as well. Have had the aerials since Cameron mailed them, and while the long low mound looks relatively insignificant in them – just an odd straight hump at right angles to the natural hillocks, with two outliers, lobes trailing off it – it is impressive to walk around and over.

The village must've been more than a seasonal encampment – the two previous digs have produced post holes for only ten houses but that is significant in itself. *Houses*, not circular shelters.

The anomaly sits at the southern end. The houses, in twos mainly, are a straggling rectangle to the north, and beyond them, running in a north–south line, is the mound.

I've already taken a look at the small cutting the Year One team had made, over a decade ago, right at the northern end. That tip is quite low, no more than a metre at the cut face, tapering down to the ground.

Material from the ground up from the first uncovered portion:

- three fragments of moa shell
- bone material from 'at least' a dozen penguin chicks
- half a hogback adze
- a canid molar partly drilled

- disarticulated fur seal bones, mainly from flippers, more than seven individuals
- four silcrete blades, worn past usefulness
- remnants of something woven from untreated flax
- over seventy articulated skeletons of red cod, found pretty well exactly where and as the frames had landed on the rubbish heap
- a very large number of vertebrae from barracouta
- an even larger number of tuatua shells forming a layer nearly fifteen centimetres thick
- a cover of charcoal, five centimetres deep.

Those last two layers are quite clear at the face of the cut. Dates: 650 BPE +/- 50 through to 400 BPE +/- 50.
A not-unusually stratified coastal midden from the archaic period. Except for the charcoal – if that is contiguous throughout the top of the mound, we have something unusual.

Which would make three unusual things.

The anomaly of course. We'll remove the protective sand cover first thing.

And the long occupation by quite a number of people. Enough people to make enough rubbish to make a midden that is nearly a quarter of a kilometre in length, fifteen metres wide, and nearly three metres at its highest, deepest, point.

The work crew have set up half a dozen cabinettes. Mine has a shower and toilet, with a dinky washbasin on top of the cistern, and a three metre square main room – double bed and desk, modem jack and power points, very comfortable chair. There's a little fridge, a jug, a microwave – think of a basic inexpensive motel room. Bland wall and floor coverings, but warm and comfortable enough.

Cameron and Bea will have similar accommodation, the postdoc Ellen Partigo something a little smaller. The largest shelter is a bunkroom with a couple of showers and loos for the hands, aka undergraduate students earning field points, all eight of them. Ahh, hierarchies ...

The key room is the mess, and yes, we will cook and eat there, but I know those two long tables will be where finds are cleaned and catalogued and carefully packed away. That is where we will talk and argue and learn after the practical uncovery work has finished each day.

It's all very civilised and guaranteed not to cause environmental damage. A far cry indeed from the tents and long drops and umukai and barbeques I can remember from thirty years ago at another coastal site. We contributed our own little midden there. But we were using shovels and sieves, measuring tapes and paintbrushes, making the odd Harris matrix and noting everything via paper, and primitive 35 mm film cameras. The technologies have changed. Life has changed. I have changed so much.

I've put the talus up on my shelf. Astragalus. Knucklebone.

1ST DECEMBER

Sitting here in a frowst of simple pleasures – did somebody

say that? – I know she didn't – a warming homely smell of fishnchips and salted oil and paper – though not newsprint, still plain cream paper rather than thin shiney-whiteinsided brown bags or twee dioxin-riddled cardboard boxes decorated with anatomically impossible fish upright on their tails and happyhappy smiles on their blubberlipped anthropomorphised faces, or, worst, those convenient throwaway plastic clip-on-lidded containers with limp sachets of plasticky tomato ketchup and black sauce tucked coyly inside – and the complex tang of bruised squeezed lemon cutting through the fug; a full glass of Peregrine pinot noir to hand, and already spicing the air, and lastly, not least in the aromascape, the little ancient musterer's stove emitting scents of hot iron and fresh black leading, coke and warm copper chimney – ahhh!

Four years since I lit it last.

So, tonight is the bright copper penny?

Lay it beside the browned ankle joint.

> Which I found fifty-five years ago where the river in spate had carved into its own bank. I took it to school for the morning talk, and the teacher had looked at it and then at me with anger. 'You should know better than to pick up pieces of people!' 'But,' I began and he looked at me more closely. 'Oh, you didn't know that that's what this is ... it was someone's ankle joint a long time ago. Where did you find it?' So, after school I showed him, and he pointed

> out the exposed bands of mud and said, 'That is almost certainly from the great flood of the 1820s. Many people died then, and there were not enough left to bury the drowned.' For an hour, a seminal fascinating hour, he taught me some history I had never suspected and a little bit of how to read land. He was the best kind of teacher, a person of passion who shared what he knew. A pity that one of his passions was my mother, who rejected him. 'I don't mind his missing leg but the war has made him a drunkard.' She didn't weep when we heard he had shot himself.

I've wondered, many many times since, how he came upon his knowledge of human anatomy. Pieces of people ...

Spent some of the afternoon wandering the site and beyond. There's a bonsai estuary where the creek feeds into the sea, miniature sandbar, tiny lagoon, just big enough for half a dozen tōrea to fossick in. It is backed by a hectare of swamp. The farmer who owns this land is couth: both the swamp and the creek beyond have been fenced off from the paddocks lying to the north. The creek is clear, its banks unpugged, and the swamp will be a haven for eels.

South is a reserve, mainly mānuka scrub. A reef extends for a couple of hundred metres from a low cliff that way. The tide was full in, but I'll have another look tomorrow morning – it is a largish reef, an ancient volcanic dyke, and I'd expect it to be in good condition. Harvestable. The only access to the site is along the beach, and the nearest town is forty kilometres away.

Hmm. Eels. Crayfish. Pāua. Greenbone, I'll bet. Cameron and Bea haven't chosen our last dig by accident.

I would've spent much more time wandering but the tōrea had been accurate – it is gusty and chill, most unusual for December. Well, for the Decembers I remember from the decades past.

2ND DECEMBER

Out watching the white tumult and brawl of the surf when the chopper touched down at the far end of the beach. The waves were so rowdy I didn't hear it, and so spun in surprise when Bea whistled. She is even larger than I recall, massive breasts straining at her overall top, but her whistle is as piercing and strident as ever, and the following grin unchanged.

'Darkie me old bugger!' her heavy arms flung wide, 'gis a hug!'

The wind tangles our hair together.

And Cam barges into us, laughing, and we form a very solid tripod for a minute.

'Ten years, ten frigging years, far too bloody long.' His eyes are wet. A tracery of spider veins make his nose and cheeks red. 'Let's have a look at you, you old wanker,'

each using an arm to fend me back for viewing, each holding a shoulder to keep me close.

'You have to be dyeing that hair!'
'Ah, he hasn't changed. No fair.'
But I have ...

The four young people standing ten yards away goggle. Then they politely turn and pick up packs and boxes and trudge off to the cabinettes.

By the time the chopper has returned with the last load of people and gear, we have made the camp come alive.

And now I sit, listening to the sizzle and crack of fresh fat bones turning to ashes, and wonder about it all.

Item: Cam has brought his greenbone net. Hīnaki. A crayfish pot. So that much hasn't changed.

Item: Bea has been celibate for the past four years. That *is* a matter of wonder. Her affairs were the amazement and envy of the entire flat, and every time I came home for decades after, she would have a new lover hanging possessively on to her arm. I came home twice a year until –

Item: the students have very strange ideas about this site. They oohed and ahhed at the uncovered anomaly. 'It's another tatau a Tawhaki,' said one, Jason I think. And Bea's brisk announcement, 'It was almost certainly used for polishing adzes,' was met with raised eyebrows and shaken heads.

Item: the dig has been funded by Jane Ransom, not the university. And she specified that the three of us participating was the condition for her substantial donation.

'Where is Jane these days? Still in Auckland?'

'When she gets bored with her island,' Bea grins. 'Imagine owning an island and getting bored with it!'

Cam sucks a legbone thoughtfully. 'She's halfway up that rich list thing. Many many millions.' He swigs another shot. The fine fur of ice has long since melted off his bottle. 'At least she still remembers us.'

'She'd find it hard to forget me! And you Dave. *And* you, e Cam. And –' but she stops there. They tread so carefully round the gap. The abyss.

Our hold on ourself is as strong
as a heartbeat
secure as
a bloodvessel wall –

Which is how she thought she'd go.

'Strokes and myocardial infarctions, that's the way this family dies.'

No euphemisms for her, ever. My fourteen-year-old self was shocked. Her father had just died of a heart attack and she's saying things like this out loud?

I must've looked even more bemused than before, because she smiled and said 'A penny for your thoughts?' and slid a bright new copper across the table.

'Uh, buh, uh ...'

'*What* an articulate adolescent,' getting up from the table, and adding, from the superiority of a nineteen year old, 'you can keep the coin. It was worth it.'

We'd had muttonbirds that evening too.

So, I put the little engraved stone on the shelf, and try and get some sleep.

3RD DECEMBER

Good productive day, test-pitting along the midden top. It is satisfying to have so many hands, all of them aware of what not to do. Just take off the vegetation, and uncover the first stratum – which *is* charcoal in every one of the twenty-five pits.

One of the women scowled. 'God, this is going to be so *boring*.'

'Think about that,' says Bea. 'Last night all you could talk about was ooparts and anomalies. Today, we've uncovered a real mystery and you don't recognise it.'

'It's just charcoal. It's already dated.'

'A tiny portion has been dated. However, my suspicion is this extraordinarily large layer of charcoal will all date the same. What does that convey to you?'

The young woman shrugs.

Another student, who I've noted because he is very quiet – quiet spreads from him, slow invisible ripples of quiet – I think he's called Ben – says, quietly, 'Where did they get all the wood?'

'Exactly!' Bea gives him a huge smile. 'This area is consolidated duneland. It's doubtful there has been forest here contemporaneous with humans. You will note the beach isn't littered with driftwood. And we have cubic metres of charcoal ... that is a true mystery. Think about that while we decide where to begin the main excavations.'

♦♦♦

We no longer attempt to uncover everything, unless there's a danger the site will be destroyed or grossly compromised. Besides, that midden would take months to cover thoroughly ...

Bea decides to trench the southern end, Cam opts to continue the northern work, and I – I wander along looking at the monstrous whale of a thing. I wander along the top.

I get – feelings about sites. Not ghosty stuff, just – this feels the right place to dig. Like the cache of unequivocally worked chert I uncovered at the Topper site. Bye bye Clovis boundary ... but here, I'm getting – nothing.

Sigh and sit down, midway along the mound, and watch the little clusters of students chatter. Watch the cumuli abuilding, muscular, pugnacious-looking, dense and darkgrey, ready to punch their way here and rain on us severely. Watch a distant flock of birds, mere black flakes tossed and spun by the oncoming wind. Watch the reef headland, looking somehow closer than it had yesterday. Ah yes, hillingar effect. Sigh. Watch a bluebottle land at my feet.

Of course.
I choose here.

Tonight, I reread the Kierfea Hill notebook:

FLY A True Moment (4th July 1999)

I WAS READING *THE VOICE OF THE INFINITE IN THE SMALL*, J. E. Lauke, one of her favourite books, but not mine because I detest New Age waffle and stupidity, and came to a part about people deliberately trying to communicate with flies (that book is a weird mix of reasonable science as well as new age crap) hoowee! but that strangely appealed. I really don't like killing anything now (I never *liked* it but could once do it without much heartache) & recalled that I had been annoyed at myself for spraying some blowies – just because they were buzzing about in the tent. And they died hard.

So I thought, Let's give this a go. I will promise to be nice to – or patient with – flies & let's see what happens.

It was a small blue-bodied fly – shining cobalt abdomen, duller – hairier? thorax – with lovely gauzy grey v. fine-veined wings.

It landed on top of page 74, where the line reads
'The shaman's hard-won knowledge arose'
so its body covered the 'se'.
It stayed 'saying its prayers' as Issa wrote
while I admired it.

I put my hand up to my head twice and it didn't even twitch.

The head pointed to the 'aro' and the ab. to 'he' (the phrase is 'he or she').

It stayed for minutes until I thought – at it – I want to turn the page now (to 75). After a few seconds, it flew into the lamp.

– Some meanings of aro – mind/seat of feelings; attend to; favour, face, turn inwards –

– the full quotation: 'The shaman's hard-won knowledge arose in part from initiatory dream experiences with other species in which she or he was killed and often eaten in order to assimilate the powers of these nonhuman allies.'

Well, I didn't want to assimilate anything – I just wanted not to be bothered – or kill things that bothered me.

Flies have come into the tent since, but they buzz right out again. No more spraying. Weird.

And I've noticed flies ever since.

Well, I admit to knowing very little and wondering a lot, but I have learned that the more I know, the less I understand of the whys and wherefores. Replacing the field notebook in the container under the shelf, I remember how I found that engraving. Crying my eyes out on the beach at Colac Bay, and hurling stones into the sea, and Cam coming by, having heard about it, and offering comfort. 'Come home with me. We've got birds for tea.' And then, sharply, 'Don't throw that one. There's carving on it.'

Who Made Me?

The land that grew the roots
that grew me
And the sea that fed the fish and birds
that fed me

And the wind that drove the world
and knew me
and blew over all –

4TH DECEMBER

Frustrating sort of a day though initially good. We divided into two teams, four students with Bea, four with Cam at the northern end, with Ellen recording – she's a neat and methodical person, middle-level academic record, uncharismatic. Very interested in dating methods apparently, and convinced that the current generation of archaeologists have got it right at last. Bea told me that an hour ago, and we guffawed.

I'm recording for Bea, as we've decided to leave the last couple of weeks for my chosen site, it being much larger, deeper, and including part of one of the lobes. All of us will work it. So, ten days at either end of the mound, ten days in the middle, three-day holiday break, and the remaining period finishing off. The physical part, that is.

It's not inspiring work, carefully removing the scraggly vegetation and the underlying layer of charcoal, having taken – hopefully uncontaminated – samples of the latter across the width of the trench-to-be. By lunch break, the sparking enthusiasm that most of the kids had in the morning has dimmed. 'Charcoal is sooo charcoal,' fumes the bored young woman, and loses at least ten minutes of noodle-eating because Ellen takes her aside and reinforces everything she should have learned about the virtues and vices of charcoal for dating purposes. Cam and I exchange looks – most the students have unobtrusively moved away from the pair of them, and, indeed, from Bea and us. There's bright chatter going on but not a lot of it is about grass or charcoal.

And right after the lunch break, the rain starts. Rigging tarps over the two exposed sites isn't a problem, and we've already retopped the test pits, but it makes further excavation uncomfortable. By two, there's general agreement about throwing in the trowel.

Problem: the mess has an adequate kitchen, but no heating. A dry little lecture from me – who I was, some of what I had done, why I had switched to being more photographer-recorder than archaeologist – didn't warm things up much. The rain beat harder on the aluminium roof, I hadn't a mike, several people were shivering ...

'Bloody weather,' says Bea, 'you know what? The forecast is for more of the same.'

5TH DECEMBER

The good thing about weather forecasting now is that it is fairly accurate.

The bad thing about weather forecasting now is that it is unfairly accurate.

Rain slashing down, hard southerly belting in – auē te kōkōtoka! as Cam's mum used to say, misery misery all is misery –

and right on cue, Cam came in.

'Geez!' dropping his raincoat by the door, 'this is bloody winter Darkie.'

'Cannot agree more. Coffee?'

'Tea for me thanks ... ah! Bless this stove!'

'And bless my forethought in having four sacks of coal briquettes flown in.'

'Hey, I've taken care of the inner warmth!'

Four dozen assorted reds, ditto still whites, Bea had said. Just for the three of us. And two crates of vodka ...

'Bless your quartermasterly socks. Speaking of which, we're going to need some way of drying clothes and people if this keeps up.'

He's clasping the mug tightly. 'Forecast is clearing tomorrow.'

'Yeah, heard it. "Otego and Southland, clearing from the south with rain about th' yelps." Thenks, I thought.'

'Snarky, boy, snarky.'

'You go away for a while and you start hearing our verbal quirks.'

'So, everybody stays inside, no worries with drying anything out.'

'Two days missed though.'

'Seriously Dave, this is going to be straightforward as. Big job, yes, but we've already got good straightforward stratification, and established dates. The kaik area is for the next party. All we're doing really is confirming what is known.'

'Maybe. I always expect surprises.'

'Well, you've found a few.' He wanders over to the shelf,

nods to the photograph, runs his forefinger down the side of the frame as though he were stroking her cheek. 'Ailsa ... thought you'd have o I dunno, an eccentric flint or a nice chert hand axe, something a bit more spectacular. You've had this stuff since you were a kid. Well, not the field books.' He picks up the little engraved stone. 'You ever get an authoritative opinion?'

'Couldn't. It's a bird, could be a shearwater, probably resting on the water. Not possible to date of course, but the engraving isn't recent. Two centuries? Three? More? Who knows? We were probably as right as anyone can be.'

'Some old, down on the bay shore, nice sunny day, watching a tītī works, inscribes participant on convenient chunk of sandstone.'

'Yeah. I have got more spectacular bits but they don't really look it. You have to know the stories.'

'That's what we'll do then. You bring two or three of your bits, that stone especially, you still got the au-ika? Chat about where they came from, and I'll fill in with foodgathering stuff here, and Bea will add whatever she wants, and the kids'll learn something and not die from hypothermia. And then we can play cards or something in the afternoon.'

So we did.

We have these dreams of a perfect dig and the reality always gets in the way.
We have these dreams of the perfect affair and the whining and messy bits/rifts always get us eh?

Time runs out
I run out
A world ends   3 noddy
Node node, I hear you say
Node my darling body,
but it is both, and end –

6TH DECEMBER

The rain has almost stopped and the wind died to quiet.

So what did the young people get from us these past two days?

A foil-backed garnet

– I spotted the minute glitter when the sun shifted and a shadow vanished. Maybe a thousand visitors had entered the chamber tomb before me, maybe more – Vikings had left their names ('Thorfinn was here' say the runes, still) and scrabbled among the ancient bones. Victorians with shovels and pickaxes had earnestly searched for knowledge and booty. Our team was photographing the wreckage ... what else could I tell them? Some already bored, others intrigued by the tiny bead in its laminated wrapper. Just names really, the names that captivated you.

A piece of pottery jar

– fired, saltglazed, a mere chip. But – I projected the stills – here is the remaining masonry, and there are the lips of remaining jars. This was a chapel, fourteenth century, and the builders had placed the jars inside the walls for resonance. A chant would sound – less earthly. An old old device, learned from the echoes and enhancements found in caves and tombs.

'And probably from drums and bullroarers,' says Bea. 'Older peoples weren't stupid, they recognised sound and effect. Now, why didn't Polynesians bring drums here?'

An azilien

– from Le Mas d'Azil, naturally. Mine has two worn black dots and a single faded red line and was given to me by a descendant of M. Piette. Thousands have been found, and we still don't know what they mean ... mine might say 'two women and a man'; it might be a counter for a game or gambling; it may be a ritual object.

'When in doubt, classify something as "religious", "sacred", "ceremonial",' says Bea. 'Or "amulet". It could be, but it really means we don't actually know.'

I add, All we do know is that the painted pebbles are Mesolithic, although the whole vast site of Mas d'Azil was used from the Aurignacian through to the Bronze Age ... the pebble, silent and snug in its little wooden box, is passed from hand to hand. I notice a pale girl taking photographs, quiet Ben making notes, the bored girl staring into – a mirror, I think. Could be a mini-DVD player.

The engraving

– Cam ceases slumping, springs to his feet. 'Now, this is local and this is what we think it could be. Anybody seen a flock of sooty shearwaters working an anchovy shoal?' With energetic gestures and much use of the whiteboard, he conveys the whirling cloud of birds swooping low over the sea, driving round and round and corralling the fish. Birds drop out of the gyre, land on the water, feed a while, then rise and rejoin the beating circle. 'So, someone on shore, maybe centuries ago, carves a bird resting on the waters. They could've been saying, Here I am, fed, content, resting a while before going back into the swirl. Hmmm?'

'Could've been bored and just scratching a shape,' says Bea.

'Any possibility of dating?' – Ellen.

'It wasn't *in situ*, and no patina or anything. We only know that some kind of harder stone was used as the engraver.'

'So it could've been anyone making it, not necessarily a Māori?' The pale girl.

'Well, the style is very similar to rock shelter engravings in the Waitaki Valley,' says Cam. 'Other artefacts from those sites give dates up to 600 BPE ...'

An au-ika

– which I send round so everyone can feel it. It's just over fourteen centimetres long, a sturdy slightly curved pin of whalebone, pointed at one end with an eye at the other.

'Anyone recognise this?'

'O some kind of needle,' says a redhaired boy. 'Weaving probably.'

'Needle but not used in weaving,' says Cam, grinning.

'Fish stringer.' – Ben.

'Indeed, and made by Cam's uncle Paki.' It's back with me now, and I slide my fingers over the creamy surface. 'He made it from a piece of sperm whale bone a mate sent him from the Sounds. Made it the old way – you'll have noticed the eye is waisted? – because he was a bit of a traditionalist. Cam used it for several years, but kindly gave it to me before I went overseas. I just fondle it occasionally rather than string a line of cod or whatever.'

'We'll change that tomorrow, with luck,' says Cam.

Your voice, saying
quietly, then chanting *Orcadian chamber tombs*
that Davy has pictured for me
Yarso Lairo and Calt of Eday
Unstan and Holm of Papa Westray
Bookan on Mainland, Knap o Howar
Huntersquoy and Dwarfie Stane
Quoyness on Sonday, Knowe o Craie
Cuween and Rinyo and Kierfea Hill

I showed you so much death.

7TH DECEMBER

By late afternoon, we've reached the frame stratum. I like the way the kids call it: charcoal, more charcoal, tuatua heapheap, 'couta, codframes. O good exclaims the redhead (Seamus apparently), now it'll get interesting, and Bea bites like a shark, Interesting! Now we know there's two layers of charcoal thanks to that tarp leaking and the tuatua are interspersed with pāua here and we have three maka lures and half an au-ika talk about seredipitous luck! and even the sampling of 'couta vertebrae is going to take weeks to go through and you say it's going to *get* interesting!

Cam gets red in the face when he's angry, Bea goes white (I turn purplish).

In the evening, Cam and I wander along the shore. He picks through the heaps of kelp (I know what he's looking for) while I just mosey. Only one storm-wrecked bird, a shag, but a sad scurf upon the sand that had been a million swarming little things tumbling in the surf last night ... stoop down to them, whalefeed, scarlet munida with their turquoise blue eyes –

'Ah *hah*!' and Cam pops another find into his bag. 'Tomorrow we'll feast ... how long since you've eaten them?'

'Kāeo?'

'Nah, greenbone.'

'O goodness Cam – when did your uncle die? I'd come home just before then, and you'd caught him a heap cos he felt like some.'

'That's over eight years ago, eight years and three months you poor sad deprived bastard. Nemmind. Āpōpō.'

He never has doubts about catching what he targets, fish or women. Or friends.

When Bea comes trampling down from the site with bottles

of Waipara riesling (and glasses, and small savoury snacks, being Bea), he heaves out double handfuls of his treasures to show her. A pile of odd kelp with barnacles attached; a dozen sea tulips, and several kilo of whalefeed. 'Now all we need is someone to check out the kina and pāua situation and we've got ourselves a feast for tomorrow.'

Bea mock-scowls. 'Someone huh?'

'Thanks our friend!'

'What about him?' jerking her thumb at me.

'He can display his special talent.'

'But we can eat too!'

'Can we feed the five thousand on that bloody little hibachi set-up?'

Bea fills my glass and raises her own. 'Wet start Dave, but here's to a fine finish. And it's great that you've come home.' She leans across the glasses and kisses, sloppily, mwah. 'I know it's been hard, but man, we're glad you came back.'

'Absent friends,' says Cam, softly.

Clink. Clink. Clink.

8th December

Bea rolls in the flat sea like a seal. She slips under the surface and rises a minute later, and in her netbag are a dozen kina. I accept them, and give her the last empty bag.

Ten large pāua, twenty-eight kina, and Cam already taken back a dozen butterfish, greenbone, mararī – I am fascinated by deftness, and he is deft, scrunching munida into berley and scattering it in a kelp lane, fastening the barnacled kelp he'd collected to the mouth of his greenbone potnet and lowering it carefully into the lane, lifting the pot slowly some minutes later, siezing the darkbrown fish and killing them swiftly – it had been just dawn when we came and now the rising sun casts long shadows over the shore.

Walking the tideline home after Bea, I notice a tiny fish in one of her footprints. The dried silvery body thin as foil, and miniscule mouth a cellophane O –

Chinchorro mummies with their sad O-mouthed masks where faces were, ashpaste and manganese paint replacing flesh –

and the sun slides up the sky, the newmint morning fine and warming, and sadness in my very bones.

The students slummock out their bunkhouse around nine, and potter until the sun and young energies kick them into enthusiasm. There had been – loud music, rowdiness, a bit of yelling last night, but that's their business. We're responsible for their safety on the site during working hours. We have a professional obligation to teach what we can, but their entertainment is of their own devising. The keen – only three that I've noted – will gain more than holiday wages and field points. The rest will serve time as long as they want. And three out of eight? About the usual proportion of the driven and dedicated versus the sheep in my experience.

It's not a surprise that those three are the ones to offer me a hand in the late afternoon.

'Wood,' I say, 'that's what I need, dry as possible, enough to make a good bed of embers about a metre in diameter.' I am surprised that they keep at it for nearly an hour, and produce a wellmade stack ready for lighting, and ask again what can they do, despite the merriment thumping out of the bunkhouse music and shrieks so mixed as to be indistinguishable, at least to my ears.

'Well, the briquettes are ready in the hibachi, and I've skewered the butterfish, and marinated the chicken and onioned the burgers for those of you that like that sort of thing.'

'You four are piscivorous huh?' Ben grins.

'Dunno about Ellen, but we are.'

'Ellen's vegan,' says the pale girl who I will remember to call Megan now.

'O hell –'

'S'alright, she's got her own tucker.' I could warm to a Seamus smile too.

'Okay then, all we need to do are the kina and pāua. Bea and Cam have got the salads and bread and stuff underway. You know how to handle kina, pāua?'

'Yeah, as a patty.' Thanks Seamus –

so I select the seven biggest kina, and carefully remove the lamps of Aristotle and the grazed kelp and (even more carefully) the roes, and wash the tests thoroughly while they deal to the remainder. Smack the shells and remove the tongues, gonads, what have you, which, rinsed, I divide into the seven instant pots ... the three of them make short work of the pāua too, after one demonstration.

'Save the pewa, this bit, the green ones only,' I say, 'Cam dotes on pewa soup.'

'So this is?' Seamus holding up a creamy stomach.

'Male pewa. He doesn't like those, dunno why.'

'You known him a while?'

'Since we were kids. Went to school together in Southland. Same with Professor Ashcroft-Morrisey,' and we all laugh, kindly enough. Bea just doesn't look or act like Professor Ashcroft-Morrisey.

Especially now, loosening her overall straps to allow her belly more room, belching softly, back to back against Cam.

The hibachis are cool, the bed of embers nearly dead. Seven sad little tests sit round the edge, their succulent contents gone, but the butterfish bones are ash. I think there might be a lettuce leaf, a bread crust, somewhere ...

I missed my chance to tell the kids that pāua have blue blood –

9th December

The cardcorder is mainly zoom lens and a memory card. I remember hefty awkward things called video-camera-recorders that weighed about four kilos and were thought wonderful improvements on the old reel-to-reel portable tape-recorder and Super8 film camera combinations. The 'corder fits in my sleeve-pocket and weighs less than 100 grams ...

but some things haven't changed at all.

Looking through a lens somehow makes what you see distant, remote, not quite real.

The resultant images are much more immediate, emotionfilled.

Taking sound tracks is a similar experience: you hear enough to know the 'corder is working, but you're not concentrating on exactly what is being said.

So I didn't really see the bones, didn't hear, 'O they're *fingers*.'

Reviewing it tonight: I am knelt by the east end on the trench, long shot, taking in the student crouched by the just exposed stratum. She is working the little vacuum brush round some object, head down, intent. I stand, the monopod moving with me and holding the 'corder steady, and move to midshot. As her head jerks back, an instinct makes me close into what she was working on. Little brown knubbly bits and slender bones, phalanges metacarpals carpals in an instantly recognisable pattern. Flopped down on the rubbish like a codframe, and decayed where it fell.

'Argh, kōiwi!' Bea does not sound happy.

'Ah, kōiwi.' Cam does. Then I remember – he's not only takata whenua, and ranked, but he was part of some tribal teach-in that led to him being certified – how we howled with glee back in the flat, Certified! Yeah! – as someone fit and fitted to deal with human remains.

'O right,' and Bea looks to the camera and waggles her eyebrows and Cam waves to me and I know for an instant we're all back in student Dunedin. 'Certified,' I hear my voice say, and they grin.

Holding hands against the sun
see soft living red
nails shine light
bones show dark
one cannot see through palms

Why do I speak and work in an adverb-rich, adjective-laden way, and she used this spare, clear, almost gnomic language? Surely not usual for a Celt, a Kai Tahu? Is my way natural for a – well, whatever group my father came from? Whatever group my mother came from?

To be at a remove from my own history: to see it only as through lens or mic.

To know my real history, I would forego any comfort I derive from what my mother told me and get right in there among the blood and tears. O I would –

10TH DECEMBER

Cam isn't about until nearly noon, and his ruddy face is greyish round the eyes and age lines. 'Veisalgic,' he mutters. Ellen raises her eyebrows and goes into her cabinette and raises herself hugely in my estimation by coming out with a fresh juiced something. 'Try it please.' Her tone is polite, dry, not coaxing.

'Already had a couple of Disprin,' but he takes a swallow, and frowns, then drains the tumbler. 'Narwhal tusk and?'

'Carrot juice, a little broccoli in sprout form juiced, quite a bit of vitamin C and a tablespoon of mānuka honey melted in enough water.'

'You know, it tasted *OK*?' he says to me, and it's interesting to see how soon the greyness goes. And how often he starts glancing towards Doctor Ellen –

no other great surprises in the rest of Bea's trench. The lone sad (left) hand is imprisoned in its protective container, with good samples taken all round it. Lot of fibrous matter all tangled (possibly tī-rākau leaves?) nearby, and two more adzes, Type 1-A and 2-B, both missing bits. Literally dozens of pieces of quartzite knives; four stone minnow shanks (all broken); and – treasure! a classic ulu-shape slate knife!

PERFECT! And, strangely, embedded in a lens of ash. Has to be deliberate. This is truly newsworthy, but I've just learned that Jane's funding has been conditional on her approving any and every *non-scholarly paper* release. Bea has been biting her lip in frustration ever since sending off my pics with her email –

Rich stuff but looks like another thirty centimetres and the trench will ground in sand.

– There's only a slice of moon up, so the three of us take torches. Black flickers at the edge of the lights, and husky little creaks that could be insects, or strange frogs. Or vegetable voices. The hīnaki are ready baited, we place them where Cam directs, and then squelch and stagger back through the flax and raupō to the creek bank.

'Grilled,' says Bea and

'Smoked,' say I and

'Anyway at all,' says Cam, 'but I am trusting to a tuna heke and all ways available for us all. Shit, those young heathens might even like eel stew ... you can still do stew, you? heh heh heh?'

'Mit curry *et al.*'

He rests his head against Bea's bed – her turn to host a late night session. 'A wise man from the East once said, If you want to be happy for a few hours, get drunk. If you want to be happy for a few weeks, kill a pig and eat it. Very sinocentric this saying. And if you want to be happy for a few months, get married – but you want to be happy forever? Learn how to fish ... any of youse disagree?'

'Yeah, it was probably a wise woman from the West,' says Bea. But she doesn't smile.

Later, Cam chops up a pewa and pops it into the pot where it bled green resentment into the soup. When we eat – potato and onion and pewa chowder, peppery pungent – he seems almost sober despite half a litre of evil water.

The first time I saw Cam drunk was at my caravan-warming.

His mum had quickly realised I was shy and somewhat solitary by nature and inwardly dismayed by her large demonstrative family. Sharing a bedroom let alone a bed made me cringe. 'No teasing!' I see her shake her finger at seven of her children swarmed round the tea table, 'it's been only him and his mum all his life. He's not used to crowds, especially a noisy bunch like you.'

My mother had not made a will. I had no guardian.

Emma Motoitoi Strathallan made herself responsible for me, child number ten.

From the sale of my mother's effects – she said – she had bought a room for me.

Her brother had arranged for a tractor to tow it to the end of their back lawn.

I fell in love with it at first sight.

Old and primitive, I suppose, just a bed and tiny sink, a table and two chairs. But a gleaming new musterer's stove made Southland winters endurable and helped me learn the basics of cooking, and the whole thing was mine own –

Cam brought a peter of beer and some illicit Hokonui to celebrate my moving in.

As I remember, I had one schooner of the beer.

As I remember, he threw up over the caravan steps later that night, and fell down twice before he made it inside the house. Singing at the top of his voice and glad I was staying. Sheepish next day at school, but still – and always – my friend.

After Emma died, and the family home was sold, I had the caravan shifted into a local holiday camp. Cam and I stayed there during varsity holidays, using it a base whether we were fishing or working for local farmers or just summer-lazing. It was pretty derelict when I first headed overseas, so I put the little stove, the table and chairs, and especially the quilt Emma had made me, in storage. Which was why I didn't mind when Cam wrote and told me it had been burned down ...

He went and lived with his uncle after his mum died, and continued to go back there for visits all through the years of university, student and graduate and lecturer, and all through the years of being married, divorced, married, a father twice over, divorced, partnered several times but espoused never thereafter, until Paki died.

Maybe it's because we bury our noses in the remnants of human lives, human hopes, human endeavours – we're right down there in the bone dust and fragments of all the hard – hated or happy – work – but I don't know many joyful, or religious, archaeologists.

I've made you a card,

she said,

dearest specialised grave robber –

and it showed the group of skulls from the Tomb of the Eagles, those nested boney eggs once hummingbusy and full of memories and shining plans, now rotting calcium, and DAVID NEMO, PhD,

Tells And Shows

How It Was

How It Is.

I place, with reverence, in full tide of memory, that Neanderthal child's tooth I found in a dusty alley stall in Peking, into the little marcasite cup, the original a hemisphere not two inches wide and found with a child's bones 'still possessing its milk teeth' in a cairn in Simonstown, South Wales, and both of them in front of her photograph. I feel an obscure desire to bow.

Merripen
life and death
what then?

11TH DECEMBER

Started with an extreme dream, one of those nightmare disasters you *know*, even as it crashes in, is a dream. I am in an upstairs stone room: I do not know the house or place.

There are wide windows facing west (I cannot tell how I know they face west.) From the north, huge roiling tsunamic surf is surging towards me, and my horror almost wakes me – They Cannot Come From The North! This is a dream! And then there is overwhelming thunder and the waves SMASH –

awake, wet with fear-sweat, wondering why the waves were phosphorescent green –

Bad news: more storm weather on the way:
good–bad news: Bea's trench, most professionally excavated, has bottomed out on sterile beach sand. There has been significant stuff uncovered but nothing Jane would really pay a fortune to know. Which I understand from Bea she is prepared to pay if anything truly out of the ordinary is

found. Which with the embargo on media contact makes me – wonder –

good news – a mini tuna heke! (Cam imitates Uncle Paki's voice, Brought down by the floodrains m'boy, summer n'autumn m'boy, cleansed and fresh –) (He really did talk like that, a kind of Rakiura Māori Southland Pom plum –)

12TH DECEMBER

Overcast, and the disquieting feeling that the skies are going to burst – they seem to bulge grey threat –

trench refilled as carefully as possible.

The tōrea are shrieking Wheep! Wheep! Wheep! no real words discernible.

Evening: we grilled the eels (smoking not really an option, though Ben and Megan went over to the cliff and cut several bundles of mānuka and, at Cam's instruction, collected still-dryish kelp – all is stored under a double tarpaulin, with the larger eels splat and skewered and hanging in my ceiling space to dry.)

Kids and us feeling a little low as the bored girl (Matricia Ponsonby) and her bosom friend phoned up the chopper and left. No goodbyes, explanations, apologies, just outta here.

'You know, she's really intelligent?' mourns Bea.

'And Daddy and Mummy are both multimillionaires,' says Ellen, with quite a sweet smile.

Whereupon all ten of us shriek and howl with laughter, cackle and hammer the tables, and get quite thoroughly merry.

◆

13TH DECEMBER
We've had huge storm surges where a simple southerly would have been ordinary, would have been enough.

A hefty grey fist of sea, knuckles folding into a white clench, comes bashing onto the beach ... o, I know. Wind and barometric pressure and the energy of moving water have created this wave. Sand and gravel make the wave grey (and the cloud occluded sky) but why does it seem so fierce and directed and *mean* a wave?

That particular one roared over the beach and topped the – relatively ancient – consolidated dunes and left foam all over the anomaly and about the base of the entire east face of the midden.

No work attempted.

Bea phoned for sandbag bags, and additional food, and another student left on the return flight. I'm so sorry, he kept saying, it's just that my parents lost my sister last year and they couldn't stand to lose me too.

I'm touched by the way the other young people don't sneer at his strange illogic, do help him with his small luggage, hug him before he ducks on board, and don't talk about him – at least when we're around – thereafter.

Is this generation *kinder*?

Improbable ... kindness has always been a chancy characteristic, particularly among hierarchical primate xenophobes, and yes, I know about Tit for Tat and the Old Man of Shanidar.

A space of silence.

It's interesting, well at least to this me, how both diaries and field notebooks and, indeed, every kind of written (sometimes spoken or other) record, are started off with great detail and beady-eyed elaboration and almost literary explication, a hiss and a roar – and then they taper off and die.

Tapered off, and died.

> *At Bonampak, a defeated Mayan scribe wrote,*
> *'I have no fingernails and my fingers are broken:*
> *now, I am no-one.'*

For years, those sentences haunted me: I copied them into notebook after notebook. This poor Mayan artist (for the best of their drawings and glyphs are world treasures) tortured and despairing ... and then, in a green flash one New Year's Eve, Wait a mo' –

it was another Mayan mob that had won, they were the victors, *and they wrote the words* –

21ST:

True December weather, blue cloudless skies, no wind, searing sun for the last four days – so everybody has burst out into longsleeved shirts and supracotton trou. Bare feet for the tough and foolhardy, sun sandals for all the rest – well, all of us most of the time actually. Doesn't matter what your melanin quotient, this sun is now way too rough –

◆

Cam's trench was almost a shadowtwin of Bea's, except for major excitements. There was an awful lot of woodburning going on, a vast amount of tuatua heapyheapy, great swathes of slaughtered maka followed by red cod genocide – and then blank sand.

Not sterile sand – this stuff had been carted from somewhere else – but aside from small shells and isopod carapaces and tiny bits of algae – blank sand. Why?

A large amount of archaeology is – despite the attempted science of our endeavour –

Why?

And Why? is a question science doesn't pretend to answer ... it is unanswerable except in very small scale very specific circumstances anyway. Everything larger is chaotic.

'Oi e!' calls Cam. 'See here! Nuthin nuthin nuthin!'

He has had the dubious joy of digging carefully further: sterile beach sand.

He sounds triumphant, and his bright red face is beaming, and the kids give him a rousing cheer and clap solidly.

But for Bea and me, knowing what we now know, his disappointment saws into us.

◆

Later that evening, he's vodka shattered chattery, understandable but strange:

– You tried dried kōurawaimaori? We used to call them crayfish ghosts yeah we did – you gotta steep killed kōura in cold water long enough to remove tails from bodies tha bodies okay okay? water has to be fresh no chlorinated shit – shell, hang to dry in the sun two days bringing in at night, right? Pound completely flat *completely* man, make 'em paper and rehang until absolutely dry – and you get these everlastin' kōura flakes, eat as is, or steam. Concentrates the flavour yeah, cool, right, okay? Anybody listening? Somebody?'

Uncle Paki is talking. Uncle Paki is trying to pass good knowledge along –

Later, Bea says, 'There was one night he had me really persuaded to try some kinda clay. Oteukuuku he said, it's close by us, Purakaunui or Puketeraki or some such. Supposed to be mineral rich, oily, edible, grey, and really good for arthritis. We went out driving past midnight. Stumbled over rockrack beaches, clambered up slippery banks, headlamps fading into dawn. Didn't exist. Well, we couldn't find it. I love him, always have, you're the only two males I've ever cared for, but – he's losing it big way big time Dave –'

we can hear him stumbling round his cabinette, whacking into the walls, from her place

◆

'gives me the cauld grue darling, pains me so much hearing that.'

O, by the way, she adds, you've got that thing, he's obviously cirrhotic, and as well as the osteo, I've got acute myeloid leukaemia –

and,

– Maybe he shouldnt've played round with that shit.

– Shit?

– Kōiwi karakia shit.

– Bea, you're an atheist! *I'm* an atheist.

– Yeah, but I think it's destroyed him. For us apes it's what you believe heartdeep, not what actually is –

and after I've kissed her goodnight, our cheek-peckkiss quickhug night salutation, and stumbled back to – well, home – I flick up Oran –

found him in the Scottish Islands – at least the story – after I'd excavated an unimportant wee crochan that had an odd piece of ogham (contested interpretation) on a wall –

Saint Oran, patron saint of nothing, ended his life first buried in a tunnel on Iona, Caithness, and was later dug up. Alive. Gasping through earth he said, Hell could be worse and heaven wasn't what it was cracked up to be. Whereupon the workers reburied him. Permanently.

Which wasn't the inscription – it could've read ORAN LIVES HERE but given the extraordinary diversity of ogham interpretation, probably didn't. The important thing was that an ogham inscription had been found so far west and north –

22ND DECEMBER

We are all up early now.

The year is rolling to an end and maybe we can feel it?

The top of my selected trench area is peeled off swiftly. Charcoal smells – different now. It's the concentrated sun I suspect. And before nightfall, the tuatua layer has been cleared. We're pretty sure what is going to be found tomorrow. Those periods where the seals, penguins, and 'couta and cod got exploited (in reverse order).

Very probably, an array of damaged (or possibly ritually intact) fishing and woodworking tools.

Ben and Megan knock diffidently on my door. 'Doctor David?'

'Nau mai welcome –'

the 'doctor' has alerted me to some kind of formality –

's'okay?' Megan glows, Ben has/is in his own steady quiet –

'so what can I do to help?'

I'm gesturing to the chair and bless 'em, Ben drops into it, and Megan swathes round his left side. They smile –

'Dave, when we were up the hill the other day?'

'Yes?'

'You know shadows and that?'

'Sorry, be explicit.'

They look at each other, nod. Megan slips off Ben's lap. 'Look.'

Photograph. Extrapolation.

'See?' jabbing urgently –

O I see – SEE!

I throw my arms wide open – to the world, but young people rush in.

23RD – A DAY OF FIVE FLINT KNIVES

marvellous!

in an imbricate line – none of us has ever seen such: carefully overlapped, unused:

not unknown of course, I've excavated yardlong obsidian ceremonial knives in Southern California which were buried as soon as made –

but after that, in a very productive time –

(Cam managed to make a slow smoker earlier, so seaweed and mānuka coldsmoked eels are our gifts to the kids and ourselves)

– we have, with energy and resource I didn't suspect we had in us, carefully o so quickcarefully excavated to nearly six centuries ago. All nine of us, with our various skills round the same long unboxed trench working hard.

- Item – whāriki/mat black decayed
- Item – several hundred bubu (none found before)

• Item – a strange cache of adzes 1-As but variant –

they all fly out,
Cam, I say, Cam come back.
Bea will.

24TH DECEMBER

When Ailsa finally acknowledged death was coming.
she took my photograph of a child sacrificed
– let us call it by the act as we know it – murdered
in the High Andes

her silver streamers and quetzal feathers
trembled   ceased to lift
but not quite done
huddled herself within the blanket –
cold and rock
stabbed through
– the drink was sour
the sourness faded:
there came a roaring silence
– a sureness too
and then
she, and the cold,
became one

o, maybe better that than the moist churning industry of maggots –

25TH DECEMBER

My mother's death certificate:
First/given name/s: Ada
Surname/family name: Wendell
Date of death: 27th July 1957
Place of death: Wey Street, Invercargill
Cause or causes of death: Trampling (runaway horse)
Name of certifying doctor: Naysmith Ashcroft-Morrisey
Date last seen alive by certifying doctor: 27th July 1957
Sex: Female
Age and date of birth: –
Place of birth: –
If not born in New Zealand number of years lived here: –
Usual home address: c/o Wildflower Flats, Usk Street, Invercargill
Usual occupation, profession, or job: widow
Date of burial or cremation: 29th July 1957
Place of burial or cremation: indigents Invercargill general lawn cemetery
Age of each daughter: –
Age of each son: – 14
MOTHER: –
FATHER: –
Marital status: –

There is no one with a New Zealand birth certificate called Ada Wendell.

Gone up south for a while.

Stayed there.

And her woollyheaded brownskinned son

fortunately found friends.

There's always these odd bits, when you dig.

A clay-sealed pāua shell in a Redcliffs cave, full of long blond hair. Well, could've been muka, except shell and hair have disappeared –

and these odd bits you get to know about –

what on earth was the stone that shone at night, called variously Te Kanohi o Tarewai and Te Tatau a Tawhaki? Destroyed by Pākehā vandals – so, we can't know – and does it matter?

As much as who my mother was.

As much as who I might have been.

There's no birth certificate for David Wendell either.

A carnelian Etruscan scarab

a cicada of jade, laid on the tongue for preservation ...

The scarab a fraud.

The tongue long-gone-dust before I plucked the cicada.

I mean, if it looks like shit and smells like shit and feels like shit, do you really have to taste it?

◆

28TH DECEMBER

Bea, plodding leadenly; Ben, Megan, Seamus, Jason, Ellen – that's us for the day, Cam, to come.

We edge our way down the middle trench.

Bea gets word that Jane is politely interested in what has been found but doesn't want to have anything more to do with the project. Within the 1975 Historic Places etcetera act, she directs that all future findings are provenance of the archaeologists concerned, and Otago Unidiversity. I *think* that was a misspelling –

O well. Catch happiness in a moment.

29TH:

Cam is supported off the chopper.

I am sad, sad, sad.

My hair stays black, my heart has long gone grey: I used to – well if not dance & sing o Sambo all de long day long – at least keep pace with rubicund Cam, and his compassionate heart, and his sister who I loved more than he did, more than I loved him.

Listen:

Listen
between the sight of a word
and the sound of a word
is silence –
see?

in silence –
see

Altieri, a prince of Italy, ordered no tomb inscription other than NIHIL.
Othello, a prince in Shakespeare, ordered death.
The Scots for tōrea is Gille Brighid, Bride's servant.

and the oystercatchers are crying O! O!

We are stories eh? Well, no human story ever had a good ending, and all the endings are basically the same. We always wind up dead. Finished, pau, kaput, pakaru'd. End of story.

Ailsa Bridgid Strathallan, wrapped in my quilt, wrapped in the earth in a foreign foreign land –

O

30TH:
Desultory. We're down to sterile sand. I don't even get fibre or minnow points or anything really.

Good clean job though. Recorded well.

In the afternoon, at Ben and Megan's behest, clamber up the southern bluff, Seamus and Ellen (hmm) are on site,

The world swings round. We sup on wine, the moon rises

and down below,
a cleaned and prepared anomaly
water full

opens an eye – shines!
and the midden throws its proper shadow
wide wide wide
THIS WHOLE PLACE IS A FISH
(and the kaika was a waka?)

NEW YEAR'S EVE

If we extrapolate:

the midden, even mutilated, throws a shadow:

the shadow is – oceanic tuna. Cam is definite about that.

The eye is – whatever it was originally, the anomaly was carefully placed to act as an eye in certain conditions of reflection & shadow.

Why?

O, I don't know enough –

It is, despite the mildness, summer weather, cool inside. I cuddle myself, longing for arms (I wish I didn't know how decay goes) to be held warmly, again –

get up.

Through out the day, with care and skill, we dig (vacuum-brush, modified electronic kō, scrape, prod, sieve, gather).

We excavate a foot further, thirty centimetres, of sterile sand.

Nothingness. All the way along and through the trench.

At three o'clock, I say to Cam, Do your call, we've had it, it's finished,

and grey Cam half-smiles, projects his mother's voice, Nau mai, kāti e!
and I whack my stick down in disgust –
 it strikes – strikes – strikes what?
and feel my whole body –
shiver –

what I look at,
this turn of year,
is
so slight:
bones of an adolescent male:
in that stain that once was flesh.
And in his handbones
carefully placed
a fired clay Lapita pot –
shattered by my kō –

Why?

Why?

Why?

Telling How
The Stonefish Swims

– Really slowly!
– Um, with a lifebelt? Can fishes have lifebelts?
    Do they got shoulders?
– Fast! Straight to the bottom.
– I dunno. (Long pause.) – You could ask it?
– I didn't think they swam. I thought they just sat
    there and you stood on them and you died.
– You mean fossils? Fossils don't swim. They're
    dead.
– O poenamu? Like Poutini? He only swims in your
    dreams so you find can find him āpōpō –

can I add to that hoard of child wisdom?
Carvings for instance: a stone fish spouting water
aleap from a shallow basin that has grooves worn deep
on the left side from the fingers of fifty generations
of grateful drinkers quenching Italian summer thirst.

And older than humans of our kind, this fish swam
unimaginable waters crowded with nightmares of teeth
and tentacles: survived them all to sink at last

in final sleep and now looks to be strange varnish
on buff sandstone. I bought it in Canada, in the deadlands.

There is blankness where the eyes were
but it is still fish –

everything changes
everything flows
nothing is exactly what it seems

blending in is a stonefish forte:
deceptively marbled and fringed and warted and half-buried
in sand
it waits, motionless.
Some stonefish venom has a pH of 6 and some is faintly blue
and some an opalescent clarity turning cloudy when the fish
is dead
and all of it causes excruciating pain and can kill –
most things avoid stonefish when
they can see them –

stranger than any fiction: even now
we are learning to use such dire poisons
to kill pain – no, not that way you cynic – yet
that fact didn't help me walk more easily on the reef –
I knew how thin the thong soles were
against spines honed and hardened over millennia.

all is strange, mutable
when you can't see/ a death in waiting

did the women realise
they would live forever?
Changed, o yes, and less human
than their captor who was –
well, Poutini: that's what he was,
one and only, with a charm peculiarly his own:
a far swimmer, Hawaiki to Piopiotahi an easy haul,
and while the anguishing clamour of his scales
made shrimps flinch, whales startle, whole shoals
shatter apart –
they also made the hunt easy, aural –
who pursued? Ngahue that story says,
Tamaahua this story tells – whoever, a woman
or the wives were lost and whether the names
were Takiwai and sisters or Waitaiki
we know the end: lucent stones, tools and jewels
that the olds insisted were fish at first –
and Poutini? Some say he still swims the wild man-sea
kaitiaki of all seabeings as well as greenstone guardian
but I fear he has hauled inland and now
supposedly fossil, he pauses in the strata
wanting utu   brooding with centuryslow grief
alone alone alone

Glossary

āpōpō	tomorrow
auē	an expression of astonishment or distress
auē te kōkōtoka	oh the southerly (wind)
au-ika	fish-threading bone needle
awa	river
Gati Laki	an iwi
hīnaki	eel pot
hinekaro	knowledge
hipi-mā	white sheep; a ewe's milk cheese
hoa	friend
iwi	tribe, bones
kāeo	sea tulip
kahawai	a fish, *Arripis trutta*
Kai Tahu	iwi
kaik	kaika (abbrev.), home
kaikōmako	tree, *Pennantia corymbosa*
kākāpō	ground parrot, *Strigops habroptilus*
karakia	incantation, prayer
karengo	an edible seaweed, *Porphyra columbina*
kāti	cease, leave off
kāti tō pōuri rā hine e hine	cease your sorrowing girl, oh girl
kawakawa	a dark variety of poenamu

kō	digging implement
kōiwi	human bone
kōpī	a tree, *Corynocarpus laevigata*
kōura	crayfish
kūmara	sweet potato, *Ipomoea batatas*
maeroero	monster, 'wild man o the woods'
mahika-kai	food-gathering place
māhoe	a tree, *Melicytus ramiflorus*
maka	barracouta
mana	prestige, power, standing
manawhenua	authority or control over land
mānuka	a tree, *Leptospermum scoparium*
mararī	butterfish, greenbone, *Coriodax pullus*
mauka	mountain
mērana	melon
muka	prepared fibre of flax
Ngāi Tahu	iwi, Kai Tahu
Ngāti	tribal prefix
ohu	company of volunteer workers, a commune
pāua	a shellfish, sp. *Haliotis*
pā-wā	pāua
pewa	roe
pioke	spined dogfish, *Squalus lebruni and S. griffini*
poenamu	greenstone, jade
ponaturi	sea-dwelling being often inimical to humankind

pōua	grandfather, elderly male relative
puapuatai	a fungus, *Aseroe rubra*
pūhā	sow thistle, *Sonchus oleraceus*
rāpaki	girdle, kilt
raparapa	eels split open for drying, also, underwater lightning
raupō	bulrush, *Typha angustifolia*
rirerire	grey warbler, *Gerygone igata*
takahi'd	trampled, stamped
takata whenua	earth people, people of the land
takiauē	a funeral, a wake
taopīpī	small oven
taua	war party
tāua	elderly woman, grandmother
tchakat henu	earth people
te mea te mea	blah blah; etc, etc
tī-rākau, tī	a tree, *Cordyline australis*
tītī	mutton-bird, *Puffinus griseus*
toetoe	various species of grass, esp. *Arundo kakao*
tōrea	oystercatcher, *Haematopus ostralegus, H. longirostris; H. unicolor*
tōtara	a tree, *Podocarpus totara*
tuatua	a bivalve mollusc, *Amphidesma subtriangulatum*
tuna heke	eel migration
tūrehu	ghost, fairy
waka	mode of transport
wai māori	fresh water

waka	mode of transport, canoe
wāta kirihi	watercress
whakapapa	genealogy
whakataukī-waina	wine proverb
whāriki	woven mat

Ka Whakatau

The following were published previously:

'The Pluperfect Pa-Wa', *Sport*, 1, Spring 1988.

'Floating Words', *Prize Writing*, ed. Martin Goff, 1989.

'Storehouse For The Hungry Ghosts', *Australian Short Stories #31/Writers In The Park*, 1990.

'The Eyes of the Moonfish See Moonfish Pain', *The Flinders Jubilee Anthology*, ed. Greet & Harrex, 1991.

'Hinekaro Goes On A Picnic And Blows Up Another Obelisk', *Subversive Acts*, ed. Cath Dunsford, 1991.

'Some Foods You Should Try Not To Encounter', *Sport*, 8, March 1992.

'Sometimes I Dream I'm Driving', *Sport*, 15, 1995.

extract from 'Fisher In An Autumn Tide' *RePublica*, ed. George Papaellinas, 2, 1995.

Writers thrive with patient, supportive, kindly publishers – and editors! E Robyn, e Brian, e John – ka mihi aroha, ka mihi hari ki a koutou – Keri